Simple Things

By
Tonya Crone

PublishAmerica
Baltimore

© 2002 by Tonya Crone.
All rights reserved. No part of this book may be reproduced in any form without written permission from the publishers, except by a reviewer who may quote brief passages in a review to be printed in a newspaper or magazine.

First printing

ISBN: 1-59129-848-2
PUBLISHED BY PUBLISHAMERICA BOOK PUBLISHERS
www.publishamerica.com
Baltimore

Printed in the United States of America

~ For John, Cameron, and Hunter ~

After a lifelong dream, my name is actually in print. I would like to take this opportunity to recognize those that helped make this adventure a reality.

First of all, I would like to thank PublishAmerica for all of their help and guidance during this wonderful learning process. In such a competitive and difficult market to break into as a first time author, they stood behind me and believed in me one hundred percent, something I will always be grateful for.

Many thanks to my friends and co-workers at FMH for supporting me throughout this long journey, always believing that I would be successful in the end.

Thanks to Mom and Dad, for always having faith.

To Lisa, for traveling this road with me and never giving up on *our* dream.

Lastly, and most of all, I want to thank my husband and two boys. Thank you for enduring countless hours of writing, re-writing, frustration, rejections, and, finally, exhilaration. You have seen me through this project and have supported me every step of the way. My heart is forever yours.

CHAPTER 1

It was late May, and Maggie Clark walked out onto the front porch of her grandmother's home to watch the sun set, something she did most evenings as a way of relaxing and unwinding from a busy day. The old wooden boards moaned and creaked with age as she stepped across them and headed for the porch swing. Falling gently onto the worn seat, she couldn't help but look around and think of how beautiful Cedar Creek was this time of year. The grass was green and thick like a carpet. Spanish moss hung low in the trees, and it swayed ever so slightly with the warm evening breeze. Lightning bugs danced around the yard, tiny flashes of yellow light illuminating the gently rolling landscape.

Cedar Creek was a small town situated in the North Georgia mountains; a peaceful and sleepy town. One of those "blink and you'll miss it" kind of places. Although most outsiders would think it was a place right out of a story book, when it came down to it, it was just like any other small town or big city...the place thrived on gossip. Gossip seemed to drift through the streets and into the houses, floating along with the humid breeze. It picked up speed as it went along, the facts twisting and turning like a flowing river. Gossip livened up an otherwise monotonous existence for most people, or so her grandmother said. If Maggie had heard that once, she'd heard it a thousand times.

People didn't have to talk about anything big...they just talked about all sorts of things. They talked about who was dating whom, who wore what to the annual spring fling, who attended church on Sunday and who didn't. There was also plenty of talk about Maggie's mother, Claudia. It used to bother Maggie when she overheard the whispering and saw the pointing as she walked through the town, window shopping on a sunny afternoon, or when she stopped by

Davidson's grocery to pick up a few items for her grandmother. "There goes that Clark girl," they would say. "Her mother sure was a wild one. Wonder if she's anything like her at all?"

Maggie had long since learned to close her ears to what she didn't want to hear. She used to wear her feelings right on her sleeve, causing herself many heartaches. Now, she just tuned people out. It was what her grandmother suggested that she do, and so far it seemed to be working. She had decided that once and for all, she would prove to people by her actions that she was a different person than her mother was. She wasn't sure why she felt she needed to prove *anything* to *anyone*, but she wanted to do everything in her power to spare her grandmother any more grief. After all, Maggie's mother had caused *plenty* of that.

Maggie inhaled the mountain air that smelled of pine, peaches, and honeysuckle, and allowed herself to remember all about her mother. Most of what she had learned had come from her grandmother, as well as gossip overheard from town...gossip that Maggie tried desperately to avoid, but sometimes just couldn't help overhearing.

It wasn't that her mother had done anything seriously wrong, from what Maggie had been told. She hadn't been a drug addict, she hadn't killed anyone. But she had brought shame to her family, and that was *almost* like being a criminal when you lived in a town as small as Cedar Creek. People never forgot things here. Things just got passed from generation to generation, so that there could never truly be any buried secrets. No dust was ever allowed to settle on fresh wounds.

Maggie sighed now as she allowed her thoughts to wander. Claudia had always been a complicated subject, someone that you could spend years living with yet never truly know. She was the only child of John and Lily Clark. Growing up, she had been the most beautiful girl in the town. People still talked about it to this day. She had had charm, wit, and an incredible sense of humor. In her day, she was like a magnet to people...they just couldn't stay away from her. She had been restless, though. She was never one to sit back and listen to authority. Instead, she made up her own rules about everything. She had pulled pranks around town on anyone and everyone. At first they were cute, but after a while they got to be annoying. People stopped thinking that she was quite so funny.

As a result, she moved on to more mischievous deeds. She constantly skipped classes and hung out at the lake. She began running around with the misfits at school, smoking cigarettes and staying out until the break of dawn.

Her parents had tried everything, but when it came to disciplining her, it had been a lost cause. Claudia was the kind of person that would do what she wanted to regardless of the consequences. She never thought about anyone except for herself...something that still hadn't changed. The last straw had been during her senior year in high school. She began dating someone several years older than she was, someone that her parents weren't particularly fond of. Two months before graduation, she left town, calling her frantic parents days later to tell them she was okay...and pregnant.

The child she gave birth to, of course, was Maggie.

Maggie's life hadn't been a particularly easy one. Claudia's relationship with Maggie's father hadn't lasted longer than a few years. Being too proud to return home, Claudia had raised Maggie out in Ohio, not far from Dayton. She had traveled there with one of her many boyfriends and had ended up staying. She worked odd jobs, waitressing and cleaning houses, anything to bring in a little income. After a while it got to be too much for her, so she would go off for days at a time with whatever man that had caught her interest at the time. Maggie was left on more than one occasion to fend for herself.

The first time she had visited her grandparents in Cedar Creek was the summer she was twelve. She had begun asking questions about her grandparents and about her mother's past, asking questions that Claudia wasn't prepared to answer. Facing the truth about the things she had done was just too difficult for Claudia. Finally tired of hearing it, Claudia had given in, allowing Maggie to travel down on the bus for the summer.

It proved to be a much needed break for the both of them. There hadn't been one single summer since that Maggie hadn't spent in Cedar Creek.

After spending time with her grandparents, Maggie, for the first time in her life, felt like she belonged to a family. Her grandfather had taught her to fish, to shoot a gun, and to drive. Her grandmother had taught her to cook, to sew, and how to act like a lady.

When Maggie's grandfather died during her senior year in high school, Maggie and Claudia had made the sad and exhausting trip down for the funeral. It was the first time in nearly nineteen years that Claudia had been face-to-face with her mother. Maggie could remember to this day the tension that had hung in the air. She could still see the sadness in her grandmother's eyes and could feel the heaviness within her heart. Claudia had only spoken a handful of words to her mother the entire weekend. She hadn't even offered an explanation for her actions all those years ago, and that was what seemed to get to Maggie's grandmother the most.

When Maggie left, reluctantly, to return home with her mother, she vowed to herself that she would return to Cedar Creek after graduation and live with her grandmother. She wanted to help run the diner that her grandfather had started nearly forty years earlier. She wanted to lift some of the burden that had been left on her grandmother's shoulders...in her own way, she wanted to right the wrongs that her own mother had done, if that would ever be possible.

Maggie had stayed true to her word. As soon as school was out, and only hours after the graduation ceremony, she had boarded a bus bound for Cedar Creek, excited and eager to set out on her new life. It had proven to be perfect timing...Claudia had gotten married to a detestable man that Maggie couldn't stand the sight of. As Claudia and Bill stood on the curb and waved good-bye, Maggie had not even looked back.

She had moved into her summer room, re-arranging it and re-decorating it to make it hers. She and her grandmother had slipped into a comfortable relationship. Although they both missed Maggie's grandfather desperately, they drew closer to each other by telling

SIMPLE THINGS

funny stories that they remembered about him. Somehow, it made it seem as if he were still alive. Maggie could almost feel his presence, at times, when she sat in his old rocker on the weathered front porch, or when she draped his favorite quilt around her shoulders on a chilly night.

It turned out that Maggie's grandmother didn't *want* Maggie to right any wrongs for Claudia. She told Maggie one evening as they sat on the porch that she had learned a long time ago not to hold grudges or place blame. "If all this hadn't happened, I might not have you around," she had said in a whisper. "And where would this old lady be then, huh?" She had smiled at Maggie then, the wrinkled corners of her eyes turning up as they always did. Maggie knew then that she could just relax and be herself instead of trying to fix things that were long beyond repair.

Maggie sighed now and folded her shapely legs underneath her. It was a fairly tranquil evening, with few other sounds besides the chirping of crickets and an occasional hooting owl. The sun was slowly sinking behind the sagging branches of the weeping willow trees, vibrant orange and red hues spreading slowly across the evening sky, and as always, Maggie was in awe of it. She had learned years ago to appreciate nature and things that couldn't be bought. That was another thing that her grandfather had taught her.

Maggie and her grandmother had spent the day cleaning the diner from top to bottom. They hadn't stopped until the windows had shined and the silverware had sparkled. Maggie had walked away proud of the way the diner looked. She was certain, once again, that her grandfather was watching with a smile.

They had been working hard to get things ship-shape for the coming summer season that was rapidly approaching. Tourists often visited the beautiful waterfalls that were located just under ten miles away. Cedar Creek got most of its business from the number of people that visited the antique shops that lined Main Street, and as the summer leapt into full swing, business quickly picked up. People came from all over the country, as well as the world, to shop, bringing in a huge amount of revenue for the otherwise quiet town. By word of mouth, people had also learned of the excellent food served at Simple Things Diner, which managed to keep Maggie and her grandmother extremely busy.

The screen door banged loudly in the still evening, and Maggie looked up to see her grandmother emerge from the farmhouse carrying two glasses of lemonade. She handed one to Maggie before sitting down beside her on the porch swing. This was how they spent most evenings–swinging, watching the sunset, or chatting about the events of the day. Occasionally they would play a few rounds of rummy. Tonight, they were both quiet, neither feeling particularly talkative. Maggie guessed that it was because they were both exhausted after working so hard.

Maggie leaned her head back and sighed deeply, placing her folded hands behind her neck.

"Penny for your thoughts," her grandmother said. That seemed to be one of her favorite expressions.

Maggie smiled and shook her head. "Just thinking." She left it at that, not feeling in the mood to talk about her mother at the moment.

Her grandmother nodded, seeming to understand.

Silence enveloped them once again, and before long Maggie's grandmother slowly rose from the porch swing. "Well, I'm off to bed. I've had enough for one day." She turned and smiled at Maggie over her shoulder. "See you in the morning."

"Goodnight, Grandma."

Maggie remained on the swing for several more minutes, grateful for the time alone. She closed her eyes as a gentle breeze blew back her hair. She could live like this forever, she thought. Even as hard as she worked here, she enjoyed it immensely.

She soon decided to go to bed as well, for she knew that tomorrow would be another busy day. She stood and stretched once again, breathing in the clean air deeply as she did so. She looked around at her grandmother's house, an older farm home with a wrap-around porch. The porch sagged in some areas, and it was hard not to notice that the white paint on the house was peeling as well. She traced a finger slowly along the cracked banister of the porch railing as she

SIMPLE THINGS

leaned over. Maggie often thought that she would love to fix the house up someday as a tribute to her grandparents. It would be nice to see the house looking like it had years ago in the pictures she had seen. Her grandmother tried, but with the expenses of the diner, she hadn't been able to afford the repairs that the old house needed.

Putting that thought aside for now, Maggie went in the house through the front door, careful not to let the screen door slam behind her. She placed her lemonade glass in the sink, then tip-toed quietly upstairs, anxious to fall in to bed.

Earlier that same evening, Nick Winters was driving from North Carolina, where he attended college, to his mother's home in Cedar Creek. It would be the first time since Christmas that Nick had been home, and, to be honest, he was not looking forward to it. In fact, the thought of spending the summer with his mother made him downright uneasy. He had stayed in North Carolina and worked the previous summer, something that he had intended on doing again this year. Instead, his mother had insisted that he return home, as his younger sister would be graduating from high school in a few weeks. He wasn't sure how long he would be staying, but he knew that if his mother had anything to do with it, he would be there for the entire summer. Although they weren't close by any means, his mother seemed to enjoy having him around so that she could keep a close eye on his activities.

Nick gripped the steering wheel a little harder as he thought back. His father had died of a heart attack during Nick's first year of college, and his mother expected a lot out of him now. He had understood at first and had gone home every opportunity he could that first year to help out with various arrangements, but now that nearly three years had gone by...well, it just seemed to him that she was making outrageous demands on him just to see how he would react. These days, Nick wouldn't put anything past her. Nevertheless, he was heading home now just as she had requested, consenting without an argument. Sometimes it was just easier to do what she wanted of him instead of making waves...he had discovered that years ago.

It was getting late, and Nick was tired. He had finished exams late that afternoon, and then had packed for his trip. Having been up late the night before studying, his eyes burned from lack of sleep. He rolled down the window to let a little fresh air into the truck. When that didn't do anything to alleviate the yawning, he began to keep an eye out for a place to stop and grab some coffee or a bite to eat.

A few miles down the road, Nick located a small restaurant and he pulled in to the parking lot. As he ate his meal in silence, he started thinking more about getting home, and he thought that maybe it wouldn't be all that bad. He sometimes missed the small town atmosphere of Cedar Creek, something that he hadn't before admitted to himself. Maybe getting back for a while might do him some good. If nothing else, it might make him feel somehow closer to his father, if that were possible.

It was late when he pulled into his mother's driveway, around midnight, and a single light shone from the foyer window. Nick grabbed his bags and went in through the service door, easing it open gently, carefully trying to avoid waking anyone.

His mother, however, was wide awake and waiting for him to arrive. She sat in a high back chair in the formal living room, where she had been sitting for hours.

"What took so long?"

The raspy voice startled Nick, and he turned in the direction that it was coming from. He took a few minutes to observe her before he replied. She was dressed for bed in a pink satin nightgown and robe that reached to the floor, her hair and make-up perfect as always, even at such a late hour. In her right hand was a cigarette, in her left, a gin and tonic.

Nick shook his head at the sight. "I see some things never change." He tossed his keys on the table and ran his fingers through his dark hair. He had meant to keep the comment to himself, but it had escaped his lips under his breath, and he knew immediately that his mother had heard.

"Don't sass me, boy." Patricia Winters gave her son a cold, hard

SIMPLE THINGS

look. "Don't think you can walk in here and talk to me however you want. I won't have it." She exhaled, blowing a steady stream of smoke in Nick's direction.

Nick closed his eyes and took a deep breath, willing himself to remain quiet. His mother had always been difficult, but in the years since his father's death, she had been nearly impossible to be around. Nick wondered to this day what had attracted his quiet, undemanding father to someone like his mother.

Nick's father had been a psychologist with a busy and successful practice just outside of Atlanta. He was always busy, yet he still managed to have time for Nick and his younger sister. He had spent time in the outdoors with Nick both camping and hiking...activities that his mother had wanted no part of.

His relationship with his mother had always been a difficult one. As much as Nick had tried, he had never been able to get close to her, even as a small child. She often left Nick and his younger sister Samantha in the custody of nannies while she attended social engagements in town as well as around the country. Nick had never gotten over the way he had been treated by her growing up, and the way she still treated him to this day.

He wasn't sure when, exactly, the drinking had started. Looking back, he could always remember his mother having a drink in her hand during parties. But now that his father was gone, it seemed that she drank heavily on a regular basis.

Looking at her now, Nick felt disgust and pity at the same time. He was tired and definitely not in the mood to argue. He knew that no matter what he said, it would be the wrong thing, so he chose not to say anything at all. He turned away without speaking and headed for the stairs.

To his surprise, his mother didn't call after him as he had expected her to. Nick went into his room and gently closed the door, then dropped into bed without so much as taking off his shoes, feeling both physically and emotionally exhausted. He quickly drifted into a dreamless, yet fitful, sleep.

CHAPTER 2

Maggie woke before dawn as she usually did and got dressed in shorts and a tee shirt. She walked outside into the already humid morning air and sat down on the porch steps to put on her socks and running shoes.

She had started running when she was in high school as a way of getting out of her shabby apartment, and it now had become an enjoyable habit. She appreciated being in the outdoors, and she especially valued the natural high she got afterwards that lasted for hours. It gave her a chance, also, to be alone with her thoughts.

After stretching, she started a brisk walk to warm up her muscles. She thought she would try a different route this morning and stay on the main roads, as she usually ran a small path through the woods. She walked to the end of Azalea Lane, the cozy country street that she and her grandmother lived on. Once Maggie reached the corner of Azalea and Main, she turned right and started a slow jog. There were few cars out this early, but the drivers that passed her threw their hands up and waved. The people here were still friendly to your face, no matter what they might say once they turned their backs. Maggie couldn't help but grin. Sometimes, it did seem funny that people got all excited over other people's business.

Two blocks into her jog she passed their diner and she glanced in. It was dark, but she could see the outline of the booths and tables, covered in country blue and white checked tablecloths. It would be busy before long with customers coming in for breakfast, mostly local folks that stopped by for coffee and conversation, as the summer crowd wouldn't start for another week or so.

Maggie continued down Main Street, then turned left onto Elm and went past the small city park. The fog hung low over the pond. Maggie vaguely made out a small family of ducks waddling in a

SIMPLE THINGS

row, and she smiled to herself.

She passed the Kellys' home at the corner of Elm and Patrick Streets and made another left. Sharon Kelly was the closest person she had ever had to a best friend, even though they didn't get to see each other very often, especially now that Sharon was away at college. The two had met several years ago during one of Maggie's summer visits. Maggie made a mental note to stop by one evening and visit Sharon's parents. She had heard, through gossip no-doubt, that Sharon wouldn't be coming home for the summer.

Maggie finished her run in the same place she started it, then walked the half mile down Azalea, working to slow her breathing to normal. The sun was just starting to rise, a definite moment when Maggie wished she had her camera handy. It was absolutely beautiful. The fog had begun to lift from the horizon and patches of the farmhouse were becoming visible.

After going in through the front door, Maggie kicked off her shoes and then ran upstairs to shower. She pulled her clothes off in the bathroom and took a minute to look at herself in the mirror. She was petite, with well-defined muscles from her almost daily workouts. She had shoulder length blond hair and dark green eyes, which were the only thing she had inherited from her mother. Although she considered herself to be plain by most standards, she was often told otherwise by people that she met. Still, she never let it go to her head. She politely said 'thank you' when told how beautiful she was, as she tried desperately not to blush.

She stepped into she shower and let the warm water wash over her, soothing her sore and tired muscles. After lathering and rinsing, Maggie stepped out and toweled off, then dressed in khaki pants and a white tee shirt. She dried her hair before pulling it back into a ponytail and tying it with a white ribbon. She hurried as she rubbed on a dab of lip gloss, not wanting to keep her grandmother waiting too long.

She took the stairs down two at a time and went into the kitchen, where her grandmother sat at one end of the long oak dining table that her grandfather had made by hand. She was sipping coffee from a mug and reading the newspaper, which she quickly cast aside when Maggie entered the room.

"Well there you are, sunshine," her grandmother said with a bright smile. "Ready to go?"

They rode the few blocks to the diner in her grandmother's truck, Maggie behind the wheel. The morning was getting warmer by the minute, and Maggie was glad that she had remembered to tie her hair back. The diner got especially hot during the noon hour, when the deep fryer seemed to run non-stop. She carefully pulled the old truck into the back lot of the diner, put it into park, and hopped out.

Once inside, Maggie and her grandmother each began their normal daily tasks, now a somewhat mundane routine. Her grandmother made fresh coffee and turned on the lights; Maggie unlocked the door and flipped on the OPEN sign before she began heating up the grill.

Before long, the door was thrust open and Carl Matthews walked in. For as long as Maggie could remember, he had always been their first customer of the day. He had been an old friend of Maggie's grandfather...they had fought in World War II together. Maggie had listened to his many stories over the years, some about the war, but mostly just stories about growing up "in these parts" back in his younger days. Now, he sat in his usual spot at the bar and talked about anything and everything–the weather, inflation, sports, politics. He was a lonely soul. His wife had died nearly ten years ago from cancer, and Maggie and her grandmother often listened to him tell the same stories over and over again.

Maggie tuned him out now while he talked to her grandmother and busied herself with filling the ketchup and barbeque sauce bottles. She then moved on to the napkin dispensers. She stopped only to wait on the occasional customer; making small talk with them, pouring coffee, serving up platters of chip beef gravy over toast with grits on the side.

Business picked up quickly at lunchtime, and for a while every booth and table filled as soon as it emptied. Maggie wished, at times like this especially, that they had someone else to help out in the diner. Myra White, a lady older than her grandmother, had worked

SIMPLE THINGS

there for years, but had quit several months back because of her health.

Maggie had soon after placed a "Help Wanted" sign in the window, but as yet there had been no inquiries. She kept thinking that it might change during the summer. It sure would make her life a little easier. In the mean time, she worked as hard as she could to keep the customers satisfied. It was a difficult job at times, she realized. But thankfully most of the customers were patient. She had really hoped and expected, though, that they would have hired someone by now.

Towards dusk, Maggie and her grandmother were working on closing the diner, working in reverse of their morning routine. Maggie cleaned off the tables and then swept the floor; her grandmother cleaned the coffee pot and the grill.

Maggie was headed toward the front door to lock it when it opened abruptly, the bells on the back of it jingling loudly. Startled, she gasped audibly and stood still.

Maggie couldn't help but hold her breath when the customer stepped through the door. He was tall, with dark brown hair and deep blue eyes. He smiled at Maggie, revealing a dimple in his right cheek and white, straight teeth.

Maggie was momentarily at a loss for words.

"I'm sorry, are you closed?" That smile came again.

Maggie quickly regained her composure, although her heart was beating a steady rhythm within her chest. "No, no. Not quite. What can I get for you?" She mentally willed herself to calm down while wiping the palms of her hands on her apron.

The handsome stranger stuck out his hand before he answered. "How do you do? I'm Nick Winters."

"Maggie Clark." Maggie held out her hand and prayed that Nick wouldn't see it shake. His hand enveloped hers: it was warm, strong, tanned. After a moment, Maggie reluctantly withdrew her hand from his, then asked again what she could get for him.

Nick scanned the menu quickly before asking for a barbeque sandwich and a glass of iced tea. He sat at the bar while she prepared his order and he watched her with interest.

"Do I know you? I'm sorry, it's just that I thought I knew everyone in this town." He smiled and shook his head from side to side. "I guess I was wrong...that's what I get for being a stranger around here anymore."

Maggie smiled shyly as she poured his glass of iced tea. "I've lived in Cedar Creek almost a year, although I've spent the last eight summers here." She looked away momentarily while she fixed his sandwich. She placed it carefully in front of him once it was ready. "Is there anything else I can get for you?" She clasped her hands behind her back nervously, unsure of why she felt the way she did inside.

Nick shook his head as he leaned forward to take a bite. "No thanks, this is just fine."

"Okay, then," Maggie said as she backed away slowly. "Just let me know if you change your mind."

Nick took a drink of tea and lowered the sweaty glass back onto the bar. "There *is* one more thing."

Maggie silently waited for him to continue.

Nick nodded toward the faded Help Wanted sign that was propped in the old but sparkling window. "Are you still hiring?" He wasn't sure what made him ask the question, but before he knew it, the words were out of his mouth and he couldn't have stopped them if he wanted to.

"Excuse me?" Maggie's eyes widened in surprise.

Nick couldn't help but laugh at Maggie's honest reaction. "Do you still need help, or has the position been filled?" He lifted the glass of tea to his lips while he waited for her response.

Maggie laughed lightheartedly and gave him a quick wave of her hand. "Oh believe me, you don't want to work here. We'll work you to death, and the pay is lousy." She used a teasing tone of voice with him, assuming that he was teasing himself.

"Do I look worried about that?" Nick spoke sincerely. "I can start right away."

He's serious, Maggie realized. She took a deep breath, then exhaled slowly. "Lily, my grandmother, would have to say. Wait here,

I'll go and get her."

Maggie walked with shaky legs back to the kitchen and told her grandmother about Nick's interest in the position. Lily finished up washing the last pot, then dried her hands before she responded. "Well, Maggie, how would you feel about it?"

Maggie spoke matter-of-factly as she placed her hands on her hips. "I think we could use the help," she said with a nod of her head.

"Well, then," her grandmother said. "Let's go and work out the details."

Maggie stood back while her grandmother went to the bar and spoke with Nick. Within minutes, it was all arranged. Nick would be starting on Friday.

Before he left, Nick walked over to shake Maggie's hand again. "It was nice to meet you, Maggie. I guess I'll be seeing you in a few days."

Maggie smiled back at Nick. "I'll be looking forward to it."

With that, he was gone. Maggie locked the door behind him, already anxious for Friday to arrive. She only wondered if Nick felt the same.

Little did she know, he did. Nick strolled outside and climbed into his truck. He sat there for a brief moment before starting the ignition. He had completely surprised himself by applying for the job; he was usually not that spontaneous, especially since he had been considering going back to North Carolina up until the minute he had walked into the diner.

Things had gone from bad to worse with his mother that morning, and he had grabbed his bags and taken off late in the afternoon, driving around for a while before eventually surprising himself by pulling into the parking lot of the diner. It had been years since he had been inside Simple Things with his father...it seems like they had stopped for dinner one evening, just the two of them, when he was eleven or twelve. Funny that it's been here all these years, he thought, and yet he had never stopped on his own before tonight.

When he had first parked the truck, he had sat there for a few moments, a hundred different thoughts churning through his mind, feeling as if he were totally alone in the world.

Now, in a matter of moments, his outlook on everything had seemed to change. He didn't know what it was about Maggie, he knew they had just met, but for the first time ever, Nick felt something he hadn't expected to feel...something from within that he couldn't quite put his finger on.

He was definitely looking forward to Friday, looking forward to working with Maggie and hopefully getting a chance to know her. He didn't plan on saying anything to his mother, either...he knew, as sure as he knew anything, that she would object, but only because she would think it would make her look bad. She knew how people talked in this town, and the last thing she would want being discussed across dinner tables would be how her studious son was working as a waiter and dishwasher at a local diner. Nick knew that he would definitely have to keep this to himself.

He knew, however, that word would get back to her eventually, as things always did in a town this small. He didn't want to worry about that right now. He would cross that bridge, he decided, when he came to it.

CHAPTER 3

Maggie thought the end of the week would never come. She continued to jog each morning, then worked hard at the diner; yet still she was unable to get a good night's sleep. She tossed and turned, fleeting glimpses of Nick invading her dreams. She felt a little silly, actually, over her reaction to Nick Winters.

Maggie had only dated a few times, and that was back in Ohio. They had only consisted of first dates...no one had warranted a second. The guys she had gone out with had proven to be rude, insensitive, and selfish...definitely not boyfriend material. Plus she knew her mother's history with men...Maggie would do everything in her power to keep from making her mother's mistakes as far as that was concerned.

Since she had lived with her grandmother, Maggie had hardly ventured out at all. Her grandmother got together with her older friends to play cards twice a week and had tried to persuade Maggie to go, but she never would. And since Sharon had been in college, Maggie really hadn't had anyone to go and visit. But to be honest, it never bothered her too much. Maggie had enough to keep her occupied and, until recently, had rarely thought about her lack of social life.

But now, Maggie was constantly thinking about seeing Nick again, hoping that she wasn't being completely ridiculous. He was a good-looking guy, a college student he had told her grandmother, and would *surely* have a girlfriend. But at the same time, Maggie knew that she hadn't imagined the way he smiled at her...she had felt it all the way to her toes. All through the week, she found herself glancing up each time the front door to the diner opened, hoping that Nick would decide to drop by early.

To Maggie's disappointment, he never did.

Friday morning, however, when Maggie and Lily pulled in to the parking lot, Nick was already there, waiting. Maggie's stomach knotted up for a split second. She closed her eyes and took a deep breath, willing herself to relax. She had never experienced this before, and the feeling was intoxicating.

Her grandmother patted Maggie on the knee before opening her door and stepping out of the truck. "You okay, honey?"

"I'm fine. Fine." Maggie closed her eyes again for a brief second before stepping out of the truck, slamming the door behind her. Nick was already on his way over.

He was wearing blue jeans, a black tee shirt, and work boots. He looked rugged, dripping with masculinity. "Good morning." That gorgeous smile was once again flashed at Maggie. She couldn't take her eyes off of him.

"Morning. You're early." Maggie could have kicked herself, but she couldn't think of anything else to say. She realized that she probably sounded uptight and hoped that Nick didn't notice. Her heart was pounding as Nick's blue eyes pierced hers.

"Punctuality is a bad habit of mine. I'll try to do better next time."

Maggie continued to stare deeply into Nick's eyes and thought to herself that she could stare into them all day and never get bored. She didn't realize that she hadn't answered Nick until he spoke again.

Nick chuckled lightly. "You act like you're a million miles away."

If you only knew, Maggie wanted to say. Instead, she apologized, laughing softly and bringing a delicate hand to her forehead. "I guess I'm not quite awake yet."

Once inside, she gave Nick a brief tour and explanation of his responsibilities, which she would be sharing with him. She gave him a lesson in running the grill and the deep fryer, in making barbecue sauce and sweet tea by the gallon. She tried to maintain her composure as Nick bumped against her once or twice in the narrow space behind the bar. When he walked behind her to wait on a customer, he would gently place his hand on the small of her back, sending unexpected shivers of excitement up and down her spine.

Maggie was enjoying Nick's company so much that the day flew

SIMPLE THINGS

by...before she knew it, the lunch rush was over and it was early afternoon. Maggie and Nick grabbed something cold to drink when they got a slight break and sat in the back booth, where Maggie and her grandmother usually sat. This time, however, Lily didn't join them. She had seen how well they had gotten along together and felt that she would give them some space, some time to be alone.

"I'm going to be in the back office doing some bookkeeping," Lily said as she walked to the back of the diner. "You two behave yourselves," she teased, her tone light.

"We'll try," Nick jokingly replied.

"Your grandmother seems like a really nice lady," Nick said to Maggie once Lily was out of earshot.

"She is," Maggie confirmed. "I don't know where I'd be today if it weren't for her."

Nick took a drink of his tea and sat it back down. "What do you mean?" He was sincere, genuinely interested in hearing more.

Maggie didn't answer right away, thinking.

"There you go again," Nick said to her, interrupting her thoughts. "That far away look in your eyes." He smiled. "You must have a lot on your mind." When Maggie didn't answer right away, Nick peered into her eyes. "I'm a very good listener, you know. I got an 'A' in college for that." His eyes were smiling and warm.

"Oh, I do have plenty on my mind," Maggie said with a nod. Sensing that Nick was waiting for her to continue, she did just that. "It's just that...well, to make a long story short, I never really got along with my mother, unfortunately. She got married right before I graduated last year, and Bill is all she cared about. My grandma offered for me to come out here and live with her, and it was the only logical thing for me to do." Maggie paused, then gazed up at Nick. "I feel like I belong somewhere now. Does that make sense?" She wondered if she was opening up too much. Some guys didn't like that kind of thing, but with Nick it was different. She felt almost compelled to share things with him. Regardless, her cheeks still flushed, slightly embarrassed by her honesty.

Nick stared at Maggie before responding. She was definitely

unlike anyone that he had ever met. He was used to rich girls, girls that were supposedly classy, but in reality had no class at all. He was used to girls that always had their hand out for what they could get, girls that didn't know what it was like to do an honest days work.

Maggie was different. She was beautiful, but she didn't even realize it. She worked hard, was loyal to her grandmother, and was strong. He had learned all of this just from being with her one day. This was definitely a nice change...he could tell, or at least he *hoped*, that this was going to be an incredible summer.

"Now who's in left field?" Maggie gazed softly into Nick's eyes, thinking once again how handsome he was. "I must have told you too much," she said, her eyes smiling. She slowly stirred her drink with a straw before leaning over to take a sip.

"Not at all," Nick replied. "I was just thinking how alike we are, really."

"How so?" Maggie, intrigued, straightened her posture in the booth and placed both hands in her lap, ready to hear what Nick had to say.

Nick briefly told her about his father's death and the void it had left in his life. He left out, however, details about his mother. He was sure that Maggie knew who his mother was, especially since she was quite prominent in the small community and always made it known just how 'important' she was to a town like this. If Maggie knew, however, she hadn't mentioned it or asked any questions...another plus as far as Nick was concerned. His mother was a complicated subject and he didn't feel like ruining the moment by bringing her up. Later, perhaps, they could have a much longer conversation, and he could tell Maggie just how he *really* felt.

Maggie listened with interest as Nick spoke, nodding her head in agreement, shaking it in disbelief. When Nick finally stopped talking, Maggie reached out and touched his hand softly without realizing what she was doing. "I'm so sorry about your father," she said honestly.

Nick looked down at Maggie's soft hand on his. He reached over with his other hand and placed it on top of hers. He opened his mouth

SIMPLE THINGS

to speak, but at that moment, the door to the diner opened and a string of customers filed in. The two jumped up quickly from the booth as if they'd been caught doing something wrong.

Business picked up again for the afternoon, and they had no time alone to finish their conversation. Occasionally, Maggie would catch Nick looking her way, causing her cheeks to blush crimson. And of course Maggie stole glances Nick's way when she got the opportunity, something that she just couldn't resist doing.

When they closed up the diner that evening, Maggie was tired. She was also frustrated that she hadn't had more time alone to talk with Nick. She felt honored that he had opened up to her so freely, though, especially since he hardly knew her. It had made her feel special. She wanted to talk more...to *really* get to know him. That wouldn't be too much to ask, would it?

The three of them walked out of the diner together in the slightly muggy evening. Lily went on ahead to the truck, but Maggie hung back with Nick. They turned to face each other slowly. Maggie spoke up first. "I enjoyed working with you today. I can honestly say this is the best day I've had in a long time." She smiled up at him sweetly. She then looked away and bit her lower lip, thinking that maybe she should have left that last sentence out. It sounded downright pathetic, the more she thought about it. *Who else would say that the best day they'd had in a long time had been at* work?! *Get real, Maggie.* She chided herself silently.

"I had a great time, too." Nick paused, searching for the right words. "I've never met anyone quite like you, Maggie." Nick looked down and kicked the gravel with the toe of his boot. "I planned on going back to North Carolina this weekend, getting a job there until school starts back. But then..." He stopped, shrugged his shoulders, unsure of what to say. He didn't want Maggie to think he was expecting more out of a friendship. He wasn't sure what she was thinking, and he definitely didn't want to scare her away.

"But then what?" Maggie asked. It came out almost as a whisper. She was holding her breath in anticipation of his next words.

Nick's eyes met Maggie's then, and he knew in his heart that she felt the same way about him that he did about her. He continued: "But then I went out for a drive to clear my head, and stopped on a whim at a little diner called Simple Things. And I met *you*." Nick paused for a brief moment. "And I knew right away, just in the first few minutes I saw you, that I would be staying in Cedar Creek for the entire summer." Having said that, Nick exhaled slowly, waiting to hear Maggie's response.

Maggie felt her heart skip a beat in that moment. She opened her mouth to speak, but, unsure of what to say, quickly closed it. She didn't want to ruin the moment, didn't want it to end.

After a few seconds of silence, Nick cleared his throat and changed the subject, wondering if he'd said too much too fast. He straightened his posture and quickly changed the soft tone of his voice back to its normal deep one. "Well I'd better let you go. Your grandma's waiting on you." He nodded toward Lily's truck as he shoved his hands in his back pockets.

"Right," Maggie sighed, pushing her bangs out of her eyes with the back of her hand. "I'd better go." She rocked nervously back on her heels.

She started to walk away, then stopped abruptly. She turned slowly back around to face Nick. "See you tomorrow?" It came out as a question.

Nick gave her a devilish grin. "I wouldn't miss it for the world."

CHAPTER 4

The following day was extremely busy, and Nick and Maggie didn't get even a second by themselves, let alone a chance to have a meaningful conversation. Maggie was disappointed in that, but she stayed so busy that she honestly didn't have much time to think about it.

They served up large orders of barbeque and Brunswick stew all day long. People were coming in to pick up food to take to the lake or the park; everyone seemed to be celebrating the warm weather and the beginning of the summer season. Maggie couldn't help but be envious of the giggling girls that came in, having fun without a care in the world. She noticed one girl flirting openly with Nick, and Maggie's stomach knotted up for a split second. She felt ridiculous, then, for feeling jealous. After all, Nick was fair game. It wasn't like he was her boyfriend or anything.

Yet.

The thought surprised Maggie, and she felt her face and neck grow warm. When Nick turned around, he caught Maggie watching and he winked at her, almost as if to say *"Don't worry."* The tension in her neck then relaxed a bit, and she smiled back at him, hoping that he hadn't known just how long she had been staring.

When the day ended, Maggie was beat. Her feet hurt, and she couldn't think of anything she'd rather do than go home and have a long soak in the tub. Nick had been thinking of other plans, though. He couldn't get his mind off of Maggie all day, and he was wondering if it would be too soon for him to ask her out.

He didn't have anything special in mind, he just knew that he enjoyed her company and wanted to be able to see her away from the diner. He waited until Lily had headed for the truck, then he turned to face Maggie.

"Busy day, huh?" Nick asked for lack of anything meaningful to say. He raised his eyebrows at Maggie, smiling, the dimple in his cheek prominent.

"I'll say," Maggie replied. She let out a sigh of relief. "I knew this was coming. It will stay this busy until August." She paused briefly. "Are you sorry you agreed to this? I told you we would work you to death." Maggie grinned up at Nick and playfully touched his arm.

"Are you kidding? I told you...I wouldn't be here if I didn't want to be." Nick's eyes concentrated on Maggie. *She is so incredibly beautiful,* he thought. Her hair, once pulled back into a ponytail, now had blond wisps falling lightly around her face. She had a small grease spot on her cheek, and Nick reached up and wiped it off with his thumb. His fingers rested gently on the back of her neck, just a few seconds longer than necessary. He didn't want to pull them away.

It was a slow, subtle gesture. Maggie couldn't control the butterflies she felt in her stomach. Nick slowly removed his hand without saying a word. She was surprised at how his slight touch had affected her, outside and in. Her skin burned from where his fingers had once rested, she longed to have him touch her again. He started to speak, but Maggie beat him to it.

She cleared her throat and spoke slowly. "So...what are your plans tonight?" She put both hands in her back pockets while she waited for his response. She assumed that he would be hanging out with friends, drinking beer, maybe going to visit a girlfriend...

"I was just about to ask you the same thing," Nick replied softly. "Maggie..." Nick stopped for a moment, trying to get his thoughts together. "Would you like to go out tonight?"

Maggie looked up at Nick, her face already showing her answer. She spoke slowly: "I'd love to."

A look of relief passed over Nick's face and he exhaled a long breath. He had never felt this nervous before when he had asked any girl out. Rubbing his hands together gently, he asked: "What time should I pick you up?"

They decided on a time, and then Maggie gave him directions to her house. She ran to the truck to where her grandmother was waiting, then turned on her heels to look over at Nick. He was pulling out of the parking lot already, but she didn't miss the wink he gave her when he turned his head in her direction.

On the way back to the house, Maggie was excited, but she tried to contain her feelings. After all, it was just a date. That might be all it would ever amount to. She answered coolly, "He's seems nice," when her grandma asked her what she thought about Nick.

The truck had barely come to a stop in the driveway, however, when Maggie jumped out and ran inside. This was her first date in a long time, and the only one that Maggie had ever cared about. Lily couldn't help but smile to herself as she opened her truck door and climbed out. This was so unlike the Maggie she knew. But Lily really liked this Nick, and she had come to be a pretty good judge of character. Maggie deserved to be happy, and if this did it, so be it.

Upstairs, Maggie took a shower instead of soaking in the tub like she had planned earlier, in the interest of saving time. She toweled off, then wrapped the towel around her and went to her closet to find something to wear. She knew that they probably weren't going anywhere special, but Nick had so far only seen her in jeans or khaki pants, the kind of clothes she worked in. She felt like wearing something a little more feminine, she just wasn't sure what look she wanted to go for.

She tried on a light yellow dress with little blue flowers, but quickly decided that it looked a bit too dressy. She went through several other outfits, then finally decided on a knee-length blue jean skirt, a white short sleeve eyelet lace shirt with tiny buttons down the front, and white sandals. The sandals showed off her pink painted toenails. She left her hair down instead of pulling it back, and the golden tresses framed her face.

As a finishing touch, Maggie put on a tiny pearl necklace and matching pearl earrings, a graduation gift from her grandmother. She added pink lipstick and stood back in the mirror to inspect her look.

Not bad, she thought. Casual–yet not *too* much so. She looked comfortable yet classy. Satisfied, Maggie grabbed her purse and ran downstairs to wait for Nick.

Maggie flew down the stairs and stopped in her tracks. Nick was standing at the bottom of the stairs already, waiting quietly in the foyer. Her grandma must have let him in while she was upstairs, she assumed. She had been so involved with getting ready that she hadn't even heard him knock. They both stared at each other for what seemed like an eternity before either one of them spoke.

Nick was even more handsome than Maggie had realized before. He was wearing ironed blue jeans and a white short sleeve dress shirt. His hair was still damp, and he smelled faintly of cologne. Maggie took a deep breath, trying to calm her nerves like she had the first time she had laid eyes on him.

Little did Maggie know, Nick was willing himself to do the same. Once again, he was in awe of her wholesome beauty. When he finally spoke, he surprised Maggie by what he said.

"We match." He grinned at her, causing Maggie to laugh lightheartedly.

"What?" Maggie looked at herself then, realizing what he was talking about. They both wore the same colors, looking as if they had planned it. "Well I guess we do." She laughed again. Then: "You look nice." *That's an understatement*, she wanted to say. *You look gorgeous.*

Nick responded in truth. "You look beautiful." His eyes met hers again, and Maggie felt as if she were the only girl in the world. Nick already had such a way of making her feel special, and she liked it.

"Thank you," Maggie whispered, the words barely audible.

"You're welcome." Nick winked at her, and at that moment Lily walked into the foyer.

"Well, there she is." Lily gave Maggie a tender pat on the back. "I might not be here when you get in tonight, honey." She then spoke to Nick: "It's my card night." She laughed. "An old lady like me has to have fun some time."

"Well you have a good time, too," Nick replied. "And don't worry about Maggie. She'll be fine." For some reason, Nick felt that he

SIMPLE THINGS

had to let Lily know that Maggie would be safe with him.

Nick, the perfect gentleman, held the truck door open for Maggie while she climbed in. After he got in the driver's side, he turned slowly to face her. "So...where exactly are we going?"

Maggie thought for a moment, but no place in particular came to mind. "I have no idea...."

"Are you hungry?" Nick asked.

Maggie shrugged. "Yes, I guess I am. We didn't get much of chance to eat today, did we?" She ran her fingers through her hair, then tucked it behind her ears.

"Did you have any place in mind?"

Maggie shook her head. "Surprise me."

Nick drove to the other side of town to an Italian restaurant, Nicolleti's, that Maggie had never been to. He pulled in to the parking lot and cut the engine, then turned to face Maggie. "How is this...are you up for Italian?"

"This is great. I've never been here before."

"Well then," Nick said. "You're in for a treat."

They were shown to a table immediately, which surprised them both since it was a busy Saturday night. Maggie looked around at all of the other couples dining as they walked through the restaurant, and she thought to herself how surreal this seemed; ordinarily she would be home on a night like this, watching television or reading a book.

Nick placed his hand on the small of her back as he gently guided her to their table, a small gesture that once again caused Maggie's knees to feel like rubber. He pulled Maggie's seat out for her, then sat opposite her. *A perfect gentleman,* Maggie thought. They were seated in the perfect spot...a dark corner, out of the way from traffic. A candle flickered on the table, causing shadows to dance lightly across their faces.

They gazed into each other's eyes for a moment, each quietly taking the other in. No words were spoken. A waiter approached and cleared his throat to get their attention. "May I get you something to drink while you look over your menus?"

Neither Nick nor Maggie had heard him approach. They both laughed nervously before quickly looking away from each other, embarrassed that the waiter had intruded on such an intimate moment.

After they placed their orders, Maggie spoke first. "So tell me, Nick, what are you studying in college?" She smoothed her skirt with the palm of her hand.

"Architecture," Nick answered as he set his glass of water down. "It's something I've wanted to do since I was a child. I've always been fascinated by that kind of thing...different buildings, designs, you name it. But my main interest is in restoration of old houses...seeing something old come to life again really does something for me."

Maggie was impressed. "That's great. I'm sure you'll have a great future in that too."

"Yeah, things are really growing these days."

"Do you think you'll come back here after you graduate?" Maggie couldn't help but ask the question. She hoped it didn't seem too obvious what her intentions were.

Nick waited a minute before he answered, thinking carefully about his answer. "I can't say for sure. A part of me would like to...but then again, I feel like I need to make a new start somewhere else."

Maggie tried, in vain, to hide her disappointment. "I can see how it would be fun to get away from Cedar Creek. That takes courage, venturing out to a new place to follow your dreams." She spoke softly as she looked down at her plate. "I can't see myself ever moving away." She slowly raised her eyes and was surprised to find Nick staring at her so intently.

"Do you really mean that?" he asked her.

"Well, my grandma has already talked to me about taking over the diner myself within the next few years. She and my grandfather started the place almost thirty years ago...she's done a lot for me, and I just would feel awful if I said no. Besides," Maggie added, "where else would I go? I'm definitely not going back to Ohio, that's one thing that I know for sure." She twisted a few strands of spaghetti around her fork before bringing it to her mouth.

SIMPLE THINGS

"You know what?" Nick leaned forward slightly. "The more I think about it, the more I think I could easily move back to Cedar Creek." He winked at Maggie and smiled, causing her delicate cheeks to burn for at least the hundredth time since they'd met. She was just glad that the lighting was dim so that he couldn't tell.

The rest of the evening passed smoothly. Maggie felt like she was on cloud nine, as if she were having a dream that she didn't want to wake up from.

After dinner, Nick drove to the lake and parked close to the water. They sat and talked for a while, small talk mostly; then they got out of the truck and walked down to the edge of the lake. There was a gentle breeze blowing, and it blew Maggie's hair back softly. She shivered slightly and Nick reached out and put his arm around her, pulling her close.

Maggie closed her eyes for a brief second as they walked, thinking to herself just how happy she was, how happy she had been for the past few days. She just couldn't believe that her life had changed this much in less than a week. She breathed in deeply, the smell of summer permeated the air.

"Penny for your thoughts." Nick pulled her even closer.

Maggie smiled slightly at the familiar expression, yet she didn't answer him.

"Hey...are you okay?"

They stopped walking, and Nick gently touched Maggie's arm and turned her toward him. He spoke again: "Is something wrong, Maggie? Was it something I said?"

Maggie felt comfortable with Nick, yet she still felt awkward in what she was about to say. She inhaled slowly, then exhaled before she spoke. "Nothing's wrong, Nick. In fact, things couldn't be more perfect." She paused, then continued: "I just want you to know how much I've enjoyed this evening...how much I've enjoyed these past few days with you." She paused and looked down, afraid to look into his eyes, afraid that she was hoping for more than Nick could promise. She was embarrassed, wondering if she had said too much. After all, they had just met. *But when you find your true love, you just know it*, or so her grandmother always told her. Maggie had never been in love before, had not even come close, so she had nothing to compare these unique feelings to.

Nick took his finger and lifted Maggie's chin, forcing her to look at him. "I feel the same way. You've changed my whole outlook on things, and even though we've only known each other a short time...I feel like I've known you my whole life." Nick paused, then swallowed hard before he pressed on. "I never want this feeling to end."

Maggie felt a tingle in her stomach, that familiar feeling of butterflies that she had been experiencing on and off since she first met Nick. At that moment, and seemingly in slow motion, Nick leaned forward and kissed her softly on the lips. Maggie closed her eyes, allowing him to kiss her at first, then she responded by tenderly reciprocating the kiss. She reached up and put her arms around Nick's strong neck while his hands slid gently down around her waist, pulling her closer still.

Maggie felt the muscles in Nick's arms tighten around her and she experienced something magical. The kiss was long and wet, warm and tender, and Maggie felt her knees go weak, her senses blur.

After several minutes, they pulled apart and looked deeply into each other's eyes. Maggie's heart was beating wildly; she wondered if Nick could feel it. She was sure he could, they were standing so close.

When they finally broke their gaze on each other, they held hands and walked around the lake, watching the moonlight play across the water. Neither spoke for quite a while. Finally, Nick said, "I suppose I should be getting you back home." He squeezed Maggie's hand lightly.

They headed back around the lake to the truck, and Nick opened the passenger door for Maggie to get in.

They drove in silence, until Nick pulled into the long gravel drive. He stopped, leaving the engine running, and turned slowly toward Maggie. "I hope you know that I was sincere in what I said tonight."

Maggie reached up and touched Nick's face lightly with her fingertips. "I know you were. And so was I."

SIMPLE THINGS

Nick reached up to Maggie's hand on his face and lightly squeezed her fingers. Then he pulled her hand up to his lips and gently kissed it.

Maggie blushed again, something she had been doing a lot lately, yet couldn't seem to control. She wasn't used to this kind of attention. Nervously, she asked Nick: "Do you do this to all the ladies?" She smiled faintly, partly teasing, partly serious. She would just feel awful if her feelings were being played upon, although she doubted that Nick was that kind of man.

"Do what?" Nick asked, curious.

"Make them feel special...like they're the only ones on earth." Maggie held her breath waiting for Nick to answer.

"Maggie." Nick regarded her attentively. "Look at me." Nick once again raised her chin so that she would look him in the eye.

"I have never, and I mean *never*, felt this way about anyone, even though we've just met. I told you...there's just something special about you that I can't put my finger on." Nick ran his fingers through his hair, then dropped his hands to Maggie's shoulders. "I promise you, I want to spend my time with you and *only* you. It doesn't matter who I've gone out with in the past...you're who I want to be with now."

Maggie exhaled slowly. "I was hoping you'd say something like that," she said with a subtle nod.

"Can I walk you to the door?" Nick asked.

Maggie smiled up at him. "I'd love for you to."

Nick once again kissed Maggie when they got to the front porch, under the light of a full summer moon, a gentle breeze blowing. Maggie knew that it was the kiss, and not the breeze, that sent chills up and down her body, leaving her completely breathless.

CHAPTER 5

Maggie had a hard time falling asleep that night, only because she kept replaying her date with Nick over and over in her mind. When she finally did doze off, she slept soundly, better than she had in what seemed like weeks.

She awoke to birds chirping and bright sunlight streaming through her opened bedroom window. She immediately flung back the covers, sat up, and stretched. Thoughts of Nick were still in her mind, and she couldn't help but smile to herself. It was Sunday, the only day of the week that the diner was closed. She almost wished that it *was* a work day...at least then she would be guaranteed to see Nick.

Her grandmother poked her head in Maggie's bedroom door. "Good morning, sleepy head," she teased. "Did you have a good time last night?"

Maggie rolled her eyes toward the ceiling and smiled. "You have no *idea* how much fun I had," she replied dreamily.

"Well, I won't ask any details," her grandmother responded, even though she was dying to know. "But from the look on your face, I'd say that it was a worthwhile evening."

Maggie didn't respond although she knew that her grandmother was curious. She wanted to keep the feelings to herself for now, not sure how her grandma would feel about her seriousness to someone in such a short time. She spent the morning working around the house, doing laundry and running the vacuum. She thought a lot about Nick while she worked and wondered what he was up to today. They hadn't discussed when they'd see each other again when Nick had dropped her off last night.

She purposely hadn't asked him when she'd hear from him again, either. She was afraid that it might seem like she was pressuring him to see her, something that she definitely did *not* want to do. She kept hoping that he would call or stop by, but the later it got, the more she wondered if last night was just a figment of her imagination, some dream out of a fairy tale.

Later in the afternoon, Maggie walked out on to the front porch to water the many potted plants that her grandma had sitting around. She was busy with the task at hand, a million thoughts dancing through her mind, when she heard a door slam. Startled, she turned around quickly just in time to see Nick walking across the yard, a charming smile spreading slowly across his tanned face.

"You look like you could use a break." Nick, still smiling, continued across the yard and up the front porch steps. Maggie noticed that he had one hand held behind his back.

He stopped on the top step and brought his hand around to the front, revealing a dozen red roses. "These are for you," he said, kissing her lightly on the cheek.

Maggie was speechless. "They're beautiful, Nick," she breathed. "But why?"

Nick shrugged. "Because I wanted to."

"Thank you," Maggie remarked softly as she inhaled the scent of the flowers. She stared up at Nick, admiring his handsome face in the sunlight. His jaw was strong, rugged. A lock of dark hair fell across his eye and Maggie resisted the urge to push it back. It was on the tip of her tongue to tell him that she had never been given flowers before, but she held back, thinking that it would sound stupid.

"So," Nick said, breaking the silence. "I didn't know you had a green thumb." He nodded behind Maggie to the plants on the porch.

"Oh believe me, I don't," Maggie laughed, shaking her head from side to side. "I was about to stop, actually." She turned toward the plants behind her and extended her hand toward them. "These are my grandma's. I just water them now and again."

Nick nodded. "I'm glad you're finished...I want to take you somewhere. I almost called, but I wanted to surprise you." He stuck his thumbs through the front belt loops of his jeans, anticipating Maggie's response.

"Oh, look at me," Maggie exclaimed as she looked down at

herself. She was wearing blue jean shorts and a tee shirt; her feet were bare. Nick couldn't help but notice her tanned, shapely legs.
"I'm a mess," she continued. "Do you have a few minutes to wait?"
"I think you look fine," Nick answered her. "But I've got all the time in the world to wait on you."
"Thanks. I'll just be a minute." Maggie turned and ran inside, placed the roses in a vase of water in the tidy kitchen, then ran up the stairs and into the bathroom. She jumped in the shower to quickly wash off, then put on a clean shorts outfit and a pair of sandals. She dabbed on some lipstick and mascara before stopping to look at herself for just a brief moment in the full-length mirror. Satisfied, she quickly ran back downstairs, not wanting to keep Nick waiting.

When Maggie walked out onto the front porch, Nick was sitting on the swing, a glass of tea in his hand.

"Oh, my grandma must have gotten that for you," Maggie exclaimed as she walked toward Nick. "I didn't even think to get you anything to drink while you waited. I'm sorry." Maggie paused. "I guess I just have other things on my mind," she whispered softly as she continued in his direction.

"That's okay, I wasn't thirsty anyway." Nick grinned, watching Maggie's every move.

As soon as Maggie got to the edge of the swing, Nick stood, standing within inches of her. He looked down at her and felt alive for the first time in a long time. Her skin was tanned, silky and sweet smelling. He raised one hand and slowly brushed a blond lock of hair out of her eyes, performing the gesture that Maggie had withstood earlier.

"Well someone got ready in a hurry," Lily said as she rounded the side of the house.

Maggie and Nick both jumped, startled by the interruption. Lily noticed, but pretended not to.

"So, where are you two off to this afternoon?" Lily brushed her hands together to get the soil off of them. "Anywhere special?"

"Well, actually," Maggie answered, "I don't even know." She cast her eyes up to Nick, hoping that he would say something or give

SIMPLE THINGS

her a hint as to his plans.

"We're just going for a ride," Nick said quickly to Lily, not wanting to spoil the surprise.

"Well you two have fun. Nick, you can just leave your glass on the porch and I'll take care of it." Lily headed around back to finish her gardening, throwing her hand up in a wave as Nick and Maggie backed out of the driveway.

This time in the truck, Maggie slid over instinctively and sat in the middle, as close to Nick as she could get. She did it quickly without thinking, as if it were out of habit, then she looked up at Nick to see his reaction. He smiled at her, that smile that gave her that warm, tingly feeling all the way to her toes, and put his arm around her, squeezing her body gently next to his.

They rode in silence, passing farms and beautiful countryside. Nick had left his window down, and the wind whipped around the cab of the truck, blowing Maggie's hair in a hundred different directions. She didn't mind…it felt free and natural; just like it felt to be with Nick.

Nick kept his arm around her for most of the ride, until they began to slow down in a small country town several miles away. He made a left onto a narrow dirt road, and after he changed gears, he this time let his hand rest on Maggie's knee.

Maggie, feeling completely comfortable with Nick, put her head over on his shoulder and closed her eyes for a brief moment, trying to place this event in her memory forever.

She breathed in deeply, the warm summer air smelled sweet like honeysuckles and roses. She opened her eyes slowly just as Nick turned onto an even smaller dirt road.

"No peeking," Nick said. "Close your eyes."

Maggie did, closing her eyes tightly and giggling like a schoolgirl. "Where are you taking me, Nick Winters?" she asked, knowing deep down that he wouldn't tell her, that instead he would make her wait.

"You'll see." Nick drove slowly down the dirt road, doing his best to avoid any bumps in the unpaved road.

He pulled up to a small cabin situated deep in the woods, partially

obscured from view due to bushes and trees. "Okay, you can open them."
    Nick watched Maggie as her eyes widened. "Nick, where are we? This is beautiful." She opened the door and stepped out of the truck, gravel crunching under her feet. She slammed the door behind her and began walking slowly toward the cabin, taking in every thing around her. Wildflowers bloomed in vibrant colors everywhere she looked. She inhaled their sweet smell, closing her eyes once again. Azalea bushes surrounded the cabin; crepe myrtles that bloomed in various shades of pink and purple lined both sides of the driveway.
    Nick stood and watched her as she walked around the cabin to a small open meadow located behind it. He caught up to her and walked beside her without saying a word. Sunlight filled the open field, shining its rays upon them, and Nick grabbed Maggie's hand as they strolled through the field together.
    Nick wanted to speak but was afraid to ruin the moment. Maggie seemed in awe of her surroundings, and once again Nick was reminded of how refreshing she was to be around. Finally, Nick spoke: "My parents have owned this place for years. My mother only came here once or twice, though. It was usually a getaway for my dad and me."
    "I love it." Maggie stopped and turned toward Nick. She squeezed both of his hands lightly. "Thank you for bringing me here." Her eyes were wide with sincerity.
    "You're welcome." Nick paused before he continued. "You're the only person I've ever shared this with."
    Maggie touched Nick's face with her hand just as he leaned down and kissed her. It was a long kiss, slow and warm, and Maggie relaxed. She thought of nothing else but being here and being with Nick. It was a beautiful moment, the two of them kissing and embracing, sunlight dancing through their hair and across their faces.
    After several minutes, they pulled apart and Nick spoke. "This isn't the end of the surprise…come here." Nick led her to the cabin and unlocked it, and let her look around inside while he went back to the truck. "No peeking out the windows!" he warned her.

SIMPLE THINGS

Maggie took her time looking around. The cabin was small and cozy. A small kitchen was at the back. There was one bedroom, one bath, and an open living area with a stone fireplace.

Maggie loved the warm feel of it immediately.

The living area was decorated with soft, overstuffed furniture and antique white end tables with a distressed finish. The bedroom was decorated with rustic pine furniture. The queen-sized bed was covered with a hunter green and cream-colored quilt that looked hand made.

She was busy looking at framed pictures around the room, pictures of Nick when he was a young boy and a teenager, when he came up behind her and wrapped his strong arms around her waist. Maggie closed her eyes and breathed in his masculine scent, carefully replacing a picture back on the mantel where she had found it.

"See anything you like?" Nick asked her, nibbling lightly on her neck.

Maggie pivoted around to him and put her hands on his shoulders. "Now I do."

"Come with me." Nick grabbed her hand, leading her through the back door and out into the sunlit field. He stepped back when they got outside and Maggie exhaled slowly as she saw the surprise that Nick had set out for her.

A red and white checked tablecloth was spread on the ground under the shade of a large oak tree, a picnic basket upon it. Two wine glasses were beside a bucket of ice, a bottle of wine inside. Maggie's eyebrows lifted; her surprise was evident.

Stunned, she looked from Nick to the arrangement, then back again. Nick finally laughed and said, "Well, *say* something!"

Maggie let go of Nick's hand and walked forward, kneeling gently on the ground. She opened the picnic basket slowly; inside she found chicken salad sandwiches, cheese, pickles, and fruit. She plucked out a grape and popped it into her mouth. "Nick, this is wonderful. What is this all about?" She looked up at him curiously from her position on the blanket.

Nick stood with his arms crossed, smiling at Maggie, the sun warming his back. He shrugged his shoulders slightly. "I just wanted to spend some more time with you. I had such a good time with you last night, and, well...this seemed liked the perfect day for a picnic."

His smile dropped for a minute, and it crossed his mind that Maggie might take this the wrong way. He knelt down on the blanket and sat beside her. He had never felt this way about anyone in his entire life, and he just couldn't get enough of her. He cleared his throat and spoke softly: "Maggie, I hope you don't think...I wasn't doing this to..." Nick stopped, knowing what he wanted to say, but unsure of how to word it. Maggie watched him intently.

He tried again. "I just love being with you. And I wanted to do something special for you, that's all."

Maggie moved closer to Nick on the blanket and grabbed his hand. "Nick, you don't have to explain. This is the nicest thing anyone has ever done for me." Her voice was warm; her words were obviously spoken from the heart.

Nick looked into Maggie's eyes and knew that she was genuine. He felt so lucky to be here with her, to have her exclusive attention.

Nick kissed her lightly on the lips, amazed again at how soft and sweet they were. He pulled back from her slowly and nodded toward the picnic basket. "What do you say we have lunch?"

Nick played the ultimate host, arranging the food on the blanket and fixing Maggie a plate. He popped open the bottle of wine and poured them each a glass.

Maggie hadn't realized just how hungry she was, and she stuffed herself on the plentiful and delicious food. She hadn't had wine in a long time, and after two small glasses she felt silly, giddy almost. She wasn't sure if it really was the wine, or if it was just being with Nick. Being in his presence was definitely intoxicating.

Nick leaned back against the oak tree as he began to eat. After a few moments of silence, he asked a question that he had been wondering for quite some time.

"Where did the name Simple Things come from? It's an unusual name for a diner."

Maggie finished a bite of her sandwich and laughed lightly.

SIMPLE THINGS

"You're going to laugh," she said with a roll of her eyes.

"No, I won't. Cross my heart."

"My grandfather always wanted to start a diner, but his father was totally against it. He told my grandfather that it wasn't realistic, that he should stick to the business of farming. And that's exactly what my grandfather did...for a while." Maggie took a quick sip of her wine. "But then World War II came along, and my grandfather had to leave. He used to tell the story of being stuck in a trench for hours at a time, and one night in particular, he was staring up at the beautiful night sky, thinking about my grandmother and all of the other things from home that he missed. And at once it hit him just how short life was, how you should spend your time with those you love doing *what* you love. It was the simple things that mattered in life, he realized. Things like love, happiness, birds chirping, sunshine, sleeping in your own comfortable bed with clean sheets. Money didn't make you happy, he knew that. So he decided that if and when he got back home, he would start the diner after all, and give it the only name he could think of...Simple Things."

Nick smiled. "That's a great story, Maggie. It really is. See, I told you I wouldn't laugh," he said as he leaned over and kissed her cheek.

After eating, they both spread out on the blanket and talked long into the afternoon and early evening. Maggie told stories of living with her mother and how they had never really been close. "She was more or less a free spirit," Maggie said with a sigh. "I truly believe that she *wanted* to be a good parent...at least that's what I tell myself. But..." her voice trailed off.

"But what?" Nick asked. He was hooked on Maggie's every word, mesmerized by her voice.

"She just wasn't cut out to be a mother," Maggie continued. "She never married my dad...in fact I never really knew him at all. She spent most of her free time running around to bars, leaving me alone." Maggie paused and stared off into the evening sky, her mind on memories of long ago. "I guess that's why I've become so independent...I've always had to look out for myself."

Nick touched her hair softly, realizing how much he cared for

Maggie. "I'm so sorry."

Maggie lifted her eyes up to meet Nick's. "I'm not."

Nick raised his eyebrows. "You aren't?"

"No." Maggie plucked at a piece of grass absentmindedly while she continued talking. "Don't get me wrong. I do wish that I had had a happier childhood, and I wish that I had grown up close to my mother. But if things had been different, I might not have spent so much time with my grandparents...and I'm almost *positive* that I wouldn't be living here now."

Nick remained silent, waiting for Maggie to go on.

"Which means that I might not have met *you*." Maggie leaned forward, her face inches away from Nick's. "And that," Maggie whispered, "would be the real tragedy."

Nick thought about a lot of things while he and Maggie packed away the picnic supplies. They had stayed late and had watched the sunset, beautiful shades of orange and yellow spreading softly across the southern summer sky. When they realized how late it was, both had gotten up reluctantly, not wanting to leave, neither wanting the evening to end.

Nick had remained silent about his mother even as Maggie told him about hers. He wasn't sure why, as he had opened up to her about most other things. He was embarrassed, to be honest, by his mother's behavior. He knew that his sister's graduation was coming up in a matter of days, something that he intended to take Maggie to, if she would come. He just dreaded bringing Maggie around his mother. She had always been one to try and set Nick up on dates with prominent girls that were within the same social standing as his family; girls whose mothers graced the pages of *Cedar Creek Society* along with herself. And if she felt that someone wasn't Nick's "type" or if she felt that the girl was beneath the Winters in any way, she could make life hell for everyone involved. Nick had a feeling deep down as to how she would categorize Maggie, and it sickened him.

In fact, Nick had been turned off by dating for quite some time, until now that is, because of his mother. She always had an input or a say-so in whom he should date and most definitely whom he *shouldn't.*

Nick hated to subject Maggie to that type of criticism, because he knew that his mother could be harsh. He wanted to keep Maggie all to himself, to shelter her and protect her. But at the same time, he was proud of her and proud to be seen *with* her, and wanted to show her off, no matter what his mother had to say about it.

Maggie sensed Nick's withdrawal and called him on it. "Nick? Are you okay?" She touched his arm lightly as he finished loading the supplies into the back of the truck. Maggie was struck by how strong his flexed muscles were.

"Oh, sure," Nick said quickly. "I'm great. Why?" He ran his fingers through his hair as he turned toward Maggie.

"I was talking to you and you acted like you were somewhere else. Anything you want to talk about?" Maggie smiled at him sweetly as she leaned against the truck, arms crossed in front of her.

"I was just thinking about what a great time I had with you today." Nick walked closer to her and put the palms of his hands down against the truck, one on each side of Maggie, boxing her in. He leaned down slowly and kissed her on the lips. He then kissed her neck with light airy kisses, so light that Maggie almost thought it was just the wind.

Nick walked Maggie to the door once again when he got her home. On the way back to his truck he stopped and turned back toward the front porch. "Hey, Maggie," Nick yelled.

Maggie slowly turned back around. "Yes?"

Nick smiled at her. "Would you like to be my date for my sister's graduation this week?"

Maggie smiled back at him. "I think you know the answer to that. I'd be honored."

Nick blew her a kiss, then headed back to his truck and climbed in. He felt happier than he had ever been in his life. He just wished that he didn't have to worry about what his mother would have to say. Somehow he knew that she would try to ruin everything.

CHAPTER 6

Maggie and Nick stayed busy that week at the diner, but that didn't keep them from spending time with one other. Each evening after the diner closed, Nick took Maggie for ice cream or just for a walk around the lake. The evenings were warm and romantic, and Nick always held Maggie's hand while they walked, or put his arm around her and pulled her close. Maggie felt safe and secure with Nick, and she told him so one night when he walked her to her front door.

She stood on the front porch and Nick stood one step below her. A light breeze was blowing that smelled of rain. Maggie inhaled the scent deeply, wishing to herself that this night would last forever. They had come from the lake, where they had held hands and talked long into the night. They had passed by an older couple, also holding hands, and Maggie heard the lady whisper as they went by. "Look honey…they must be newlyweds."

Maggie couldn't help but smile, wondering if Nick had heard, but afraid to look up at him to see. She had grown so close to Nick lately and she sometimes wondered where this would all lead.

Little did Maggie know, Nick had also heard what the lady had said. He swelled with pride at the thought of being by Maggie's side forever, and was glad that a stranger had noticed their affection for one another.

Now, standing on the porch steps, Maggie looked into Nick's eyes and knew that she had to let her feelings be known. She heard the faint rumble of thunder and the wind picked up, blowing her hair softly around her shoulders. "Nick, I feel so safe with you…like we belong together." She smiled softly, warming Nick's heart.

Nick returned the smile and stared attentively into Maggie's eyes. He reached down and clasped both of her hands. "I feel the same way. I don't know what I would do without you, Maggie." He paused, collecting his thoughts, then continued: "I know I've told you before, but I'll say it again. These past few weeks with you have been the best I've ever known."

Maggie quickly agreed with him. "For me too." She squeezed Nick's hands and stepped a little closer to him, leaving but a small space between them. "The feelings I have for you are incredible..." Maggie looked up at the sky as she paused for a moment, thinking. "I never knew what it was like to care this much for another person."

Nick felt relief wash over him as he heard these words. "You have no idea how that makes me feel, Maggie. I've been waiting my whole life to meet someone like you, even though I never realized it."

Just then thunder boomed loudly and rain began coming down in torrents. Nick and Maggie, standing on the porch steps, were quickly soaked, but they didn't seem to notice. All they could see in the world right now, the only thing they cared about, was each other. After a bolt of lightning struck a little too closely, Maggie jumped, then told Nick that he'd better come in or get going, one of the two.

As much as Nick wanted to go inside, he knew that it was late and he had to get home. He also knew that if he went in he wouldn't want to leave. He quickly kissed Maggie goodbye, then ran to his truck, rain continuing to pelt him as he did so.

Maggie stood on the porch and watched until Nick was safely in his truck before she turned to go inside. She thought for a minute she had heard Nick shout, "I love you" before he slammed his door, but she wasn't quite sure.

Lily had agreed to close the diner early on Saturday evening so Maggie and Nick could both attend Nick's sister's graduation and party. She hated to do it, as business was especially good this year. But she knew how much it meant to Maggie to be able to go and spend the evening with Nick, and she wouldn't be able to run the diner by herself for the entire afternoon.

Lily really thought a lot of Nick and appreciated the kind way he treated Maggie, and she had noticed a whole change in Maggie's demeanor since she had been spending time with Nick. Several of Lily's card-playing friends had mentioned that they had seen the couple around town, and they asked Lily what her feelings were about the relationship. She told them exactly how she felt...that if it was what Maggie wanted, then she deserved it.

Some of her friends weren't so sure. "I don't know," Helen Lang had said just the other night. "They just seem mighty chummy after such a short time."

"Like you're one to talk," Ruth Anne chided. "You and Ralph knew each other about two weeks before you were *married*." The whole group laughed at that one, and all Helen could do was shake her head and join in the laughter.

"It's the boy's mother you need to watch out for." Rachel, ordinarily the quiet one of the group, spoke up. "She would stab her best friend in the back and never give it a second thought." A few others agreed, then the conversation quickly changed to the fire hall bingo game scheduled for next week.

Lily continued to play the game, but her mind was on Rachel's statement. She had often wondered if Patricia Winters had changed her ways. Her daughter Claudia had gone to school with Patricia. They weren't close; in fact, they had had several run-ins with each other years ago, mostly over young men. Lily just remembered having a very bad feeling about Patricia's character.

It took her a few days after Nick started working at the diner before she realized that Nick was Patricia's son. Oh, he was wonderful all right, but only because he had taken after his father, who had been a very kind and generous man. Lily, as well as most people around town, had often wondered how the two of them had ended up together, such opposites they were. She also wondered if Patricia was aware of her son working at the diner.

Now, Lily worked on cleaning up the kitchen at home while Maggie was upstairs tearing her closet apart for something to wear to tomorrow night's graduation. Lily hadn't spoken to Maggie about her feelings toward Patricia Winters, nor did she plan to. It had been a long time, and people could change. Lily didn't feel that she had any room to judge anyone, nor was it her place to put pre-conceived ideas into Maggie's head. No, anything that Maggie found out regarding Patricia Winters would be all on her own, that was for sure.

CHAPTER 7

For reasons that she wasn't quite sure of, Maggie was nervous about meeting Nick's mother and sister. She debated for days over what to wear, ripping through her closet and trying on outfit after outfit. Finally, on Friday evening, she borrowed her grandmother's truck and went in to town, rushing into Jasper's just minutes before they closed. She quickly selected an ivory sun dress with spaghetti straps, a matching short-sleeved jacket, and matching sandals. She also picked out a small gold bracelet and had it gift-wrapped for Nick's sister.

Saturday, the diner closed early as planned and Maggie hurried home quickly to get ready. After showering, she carefully put on her new dress. She curled the ends of her hair and applied a little more make-up than usual. She still felt uneasy, but was excited all the same.

Nick arrived promptly at five o'clock, looking more handsome than Maggie had seen him yet, wearing black dress pants and a white dress shirt. Maggie was speechless for a moment, and Nick filled the silence by kissing her on the cheek and telling her how wonderful she looked. Maggie quickly returned the compliment.

On the ride to the city auditorium, Maggie sat next to Nick, a thousand thoughts going through her mind. She clenched her fists together tightly in her lap, waves of apprehension rising to the back of her throat. *What if they don't like me?* she wondered. *What if Mrs. Winters doesn't approve of my relationship with Nick?* Although she hadn't spoken the thought out loud to anyone, it was something that entered her mind frequently.

She wondered to herself if Mrs. Winters had known her mother at all. If she had, then she was sure to know what kind of person Claudia had been. She didn't want anything to cause Mrs. Winters to think negatively about her. She prayed silently that Mrs. Winters would like her, that she would take the time to get to know her and disregard anything that she may have heard about her mother.

Nick, as if sensing Maggie's uncertainty, reached over and squeezed her hand. "You okay?"

Maggie swallowed hard, trying to fight back the lump in her throat. She nodded slowly before she spoke. "Sure, I'm fine. Why do you ask?"

"You seem quiet, that's all."

"Do I?" Maggie asked. She tossed her hair over one shoulder and looked down at her fingers entwined with Nick's. "I guess I'm just anxious to meet your family." She paused, then added: "I really haven't heard much about them."

The muscles in Nick's neck tensed suddenly, but he didn't think that Maggie had noticed. At least he hoped not. He answered quickly with a lighthearted laugh. "What's to tell? My sister, Samantha, is almost four years younger than I am. Looks nothing like me. We used to be close, until I went off to college and she to high school. You know how fast people can drift apart." He cleared his throat, concentrating on his driving. "We don't get much time to spend together, but we get along fine."

Maggie waited for Nick for continue, but he remained silent, apparently deep in thought. "And your mother?" Maggie asked innocently. "What's she like?"

Nick's heart was racing as he thought about his answer to the question he had been anticipating for quite some time now. "She...she's a very busy woman."

Maggie sat in silence, watching the traffic and waiting for Nick to continue.

Nick gripped the steering wheel a little harder as he pulled in to the packed auditorium parking lot. He wanted to tell Maggie the truth, that he literally couldn't stand to be in the same room as his mother, but he didn't.

His thoughts drifted back to an unpleasant day not long before his father died. Nick had found out, by accident, that his mother had

had an affair with a man much younger than she was. It had been his senior year of high school, and as most seniors do at some point, he was skipping school to go to Dry Lake for the day and hang out with his friends. As his friend Jeff had pulled his Camaro into a tight spot on the overlook, he saw movement in a car close to them. He got out of the car slowly and strained his eyes to get a better look, instantly identifying the profile of his mother and a new young lawyer that had recently moved to town. He ducked quickly around the other side of the car.

"What's the matter?" Jeff asked. "You look like you've seen a ghost."

Feeling queasy, Nick closed his eyes and leaned against the car, the sun hot on his neck. Sweat trickled down the back of his shirt.

"Nothing." He shrugged and reached in the trunk to grab the small cooler he had brought along. "Let's get down to the lake."

The image had never left his mind. His mother had acted nonchalant that afternoon, and all Nick could think of was her kissing that lawyer. He had debated for weeks about whether or not he should tell his father, but in the end decided that it wasn't his place.

His sister had told him later that his parents had been arguing the night his father had his heart attack. She distinctly remembered hearing her father mention that young lawyer's name. Nick knew, without a doubt, that his father had found out about the affair and it had contributed to his death. Whether his mother would ever admit to it or not, Nick knew that this much was true.

Nick also knew that he could trust Maggie with this information, but he still to this day felt sick about it. He was sure that one day he would be ready to share it with her, just not now. So in the mean time, he tried to say as little as possible about his mother.

Nick was spared from further conversation as they were directed to a parking spot at the back of the lot. Together, Nick and Maggie walked toward the crowded auditorium doors, anxious to find a seat before the ceremony started.

Nick grabbed Maggie's hand tightly as they wove their way through the crowd. Seating was on a first-come, first-served basis,

SIMPLE THINGS

so Nick led Maggie to a couple of seats in the nose-bleed section, about the only thing that was left. Maggie recognized several people in the crowd–friends of Lily's, customers of the diner. She smiled and waved at everyone she saw, proud to be seen with Nick.

"Where is your mother sitting?" Maggie had to speak loudly over the roar of conversation all around them.

"I'm not sure. We'll just sit up here, and we'll see her back at the house later."

Maggie nodded in response. Nick had mentioned earlier in the week that his mother was having a little get-together at their home after the ceremony.

"Won't she be expecting you to sit with her?"

"I doubt it," Nick responded. "We really didn't talk about it, so it's no big deal."

Maggie nodded once again; then the familiar notes of "Pomp and Circumstance" began. Maggie and Nick both sat back and watched as the Cedar Creek graduating class made their way down the center aisle of the auditorium to take their seats.

Patricia Winters watched as her son led a beautiful blonde by the hand through the thick crowd. She was stunned at first, then that reaction was replaced by anger. *How dare he!* As long as Nick had been dating, he knew the unspoken rule: always, *always*, get prior approval from his mother. Patricia was not a person that enjoyed surprises, especially of this magnitude.

Afraid that someone would see her looking less than together, Patricia quickly sucked in her breath and stood up straight. She waved a perfectly manicured hand at someone that called her name from two rows ahead. Feeling a tap on her shoulder, Patricia turned around quickly, coming face to face with Stella Davenport. Stella was a woman in Patricia's social circle, in her mid-fifties, and always trying to stir something up. Patricia had come to despise her annoying voice, and she shuddered now as she realized she couldn't get away from Stella at this moment.

"Did you see *Nicholas?*" Stella spoke in a slow, southern drawl.

Patricia felt herself rising up to her full height, her spine rigid. "Yes, he's here." Patricia cleared her throat. "And what about him?" She absentmindedly toyed with the cultured strand of pearls that clung to her throat.

"Well, I assumed you knew, but I can tell that you had no idea." Stella covered her mouth with a dainty hand, trying to stifle a giggle. "That's *her*."

"Who?" Patricia stared at Stella, her lips pursed, hand on hip.

Stella leaned over to Patricia, her perfume heavy and thick. Patricia resisted the urge to gag. "That's the Clark girl. You know... *Claudia's daughter*."

Patricia felt as if she had been slapped in the face. She felt her blood rush to her feet; her knees went weak. She took a deep breath before she responded slowly. "Well of course she is." She continued to stare down at Stella, her eyes blazing. She didn't want to appear as if she didn't already know this information.

Stella, obviously disappointed that she wasn't the bearer of bad news to Patricia, turned to walk away just as the ceremony began.

Patricia could barely concentrate during the graduation, and almost missed Samantha entirely as she walked across the stage to receive her diploma. She clapped politely along with everyone else, but she couldn't focus her attention, given the news she had just been handed.

Claudia Clark. Now there's a name I haven't heard in years. Patricia suddenly remembered the old days, her high school days, and thought about how much she had *hated* Claudia. She had hated her for all the perfect reasons: Claudia was wild, a free spirit. She was blond, she was beautiful...and most importantly, she had stolen Patricia's boyfriend.

Patricia felt warm all over, and she used her program guide to fan herself uneasily as the long-forgotten details quickly emerged to the surface. She remembered that she had been totally, *completely*, in love with Ray Hughes when he had dumped her abruptly. Patricia had quickly discovered the basis for his hasty departure: Claudia Clark.

SIMPLE THINGS

Patricia had gone ballistic when she found out. She had called Claudia's home, showed up on her doorstep, even. She was furious that she had been discarded so easily; replaced by someone that she felt was entirely beneath her.

Her ranting and raving had proved futile, however. Ray and Claudia ran off together, but from what she heard months later, it hadn't lasted either. Patricia had gained some satisfaction in that fact, although she no longer wanted Ray back. She had gone on to marry Michael Winters, someone she married on the rebound but had never truly loved. Patricia had grown to accept her life with Michael, given the generous lifestyle she was able to lead because of it. She went on to have two children with him; doing her best to forget about the love she had lost so long ago.

Rumor also had it that Claudia had gotten pregnant and had a child by Ray, this girl that now lived with Claudia's mother. Patricia felt anger and disgust that this could possibly be the girl Nick was clinging to so lovingly.

Patricia's thoughts came back to the present as she realized that people around her were standing and applauding. She joined them by rising slowly, still not trusting her weak knees. With a few simple words from the high school principal, the ceremony was over. Graduation caps flew through the air, confetti sprayed in every direction. Patricia, tight-lipped, grabbed her purse from her seat and clutched it firmly under her arm.

She looked around, trying to quickly pan the crowd for a glimpse of her son. Then she spotted him. She once again felt herself straighten her posture, felt her spine stiffen. She thought quickly of how she could handle this situation tactfully. She smoothed the palm of her hand over her perfectly groomed hair and pasted on her famous smile. Nick, with his blond-haired beauty in tow, was headed right for her.

CHAPTER 8

Maggie felt her heart racing as she approached Mrs. Winters. She squeezed Nick's hand tightly, and he squeezed hers back, letting her know that he was aware of her insecurity, not to worry. He winked at her as she looked up at him, and Maggie felt herself relax a bit as they closed the gap slowly between themselves and Nick's mother.

She absorbed every detail about Mrs. Winters as they made their way over to her. She was tall, perfectly groomed in every possible way. Her hair, make-up, and nails were salon perfect. Her powder blue business suit was obviously tailor-made. She was smiling broadly as Nick and Maggie walked up, and Maggie was struck by how approachable she seemed.

"Well, hello there, son," Patricia said. "I saved you a seat, but you were late." Quickly turning her attention toward Maggie, she spoke again. "Who do we have here?" Patricia forced a smile. She was struck by how much Maggie resembled her mother, only she was much more beautiful, if that were possible.

Nick cleared his throat before performing the introductions. He was shocked at the casual demeanor his mother was presenting, a style of speaking that he was not accustomed to witnessing. She passed herself off as being very pleasant, and at this Nick was astonished "Mother, this is Maggie Clark. Maggie, my mother." Both ladies reached out a hand and shook the other's delicately.

"It's a pleasure to meet you, Mrs. Winters." Maggie was genuine, happy to finally meet the mother of the man she was quickly falling for.

"Please, call me Patricia."

"Okay..." Maggie responded nervously. "Patricia, then."

"You're Claudia's daughter, right?"

Maggie smiled and nodded her head. "Um, yes I am. Do you

know my mother?" She held her breath while biting gently on her lower lip, unsure of what answer she wanted to hear.

"Oh, only vaguely," Patricia responded with a flip of her hand. "It's been a long time." She paused, then added: "And what is your father's name...Ralph, was it?" Patricia pretended to have no knowledge of the situation.

"Ray," Maggie responded. "His name was...*is* Ray."

Patricia felt a punch in her stomach as soon as she heard these words that she had fully expected to hear anyway. She gripped the chair in front of her until her knuckles turned white. She swallowed hard before she responded. "I remember now. It *has* been a long time." She felt anger and resentment boiling inside her but willed herself to control it. Then, turning slowly to Nick, she spoke abruptly: "I'll go and get your sister and we'll meet you back at the house. We have guests to entertain."

Nick wondered, as he drove with Maggie to his home, just what was up his mother's sleeve. He had detected something unusual in her tone that he couldn't quite put his finger on. Whatever it was, he planned on finding out as soon as possible.

Maggie talked non-stop on the way to the graduation celebration, which Nick was grateful for. Nick just nodded and smiled at Maggie. He reached over and squeezed her hand.

"I'm glad you're here with me, Maggie. I hope you don't mind hanging out at the house for a little while. We won't stay long...as soon as I feel that we've mingled enough, we can take off. Where ever you want to go, okay?"

"Okay." She paused for a minute. "I've got an idea."

"Oh yeah?" Nick raised his eyebrows, a sly grin on his face. "And what would that be?"

"Well I guess you'll just have to wait and see, won't you?" Maggie grinned back, flirting openly.

Maggie was introduced to Nick's sister at the house. She had brown hair and green eyes and looked nothing like Nick, just like he had said before. Maggie presented the wrapped present to her, which

Samantha thanked her for and placed on a table among the other gifts before turning away to join her friends.

Nick showed Maggie around the house and grounds before very many people arrived. Although Nick had sheepishly warned Maggie earlier that his house "was a little on the large side," nothing prepared her for the actual thing. Nick showed her through the inside first, which was decorated with exquisite items that had obviously come from all over the world. Large paintings lined the foyer, all signed with famous signatures. The outside had a pool, tennis court, and a horse stable. Maggie stared at everything in amazement, unable to imagine living in a place even half that size.

Nick then showed Maggie to the back lawn, where a white tent was set up. Balloons and signs hung everywhere that said, "CONGRATULATIONS, SAMANTHA!!" Inside the tent, Maggie found table after table of food: shrimp, crab cakes, sandwiches, cheese, fruit, wine, and punch. Her mouth fell open when she saw the mounds of delicious food in front of them. It was the most incredible thing she had ever seen.

Nick noticed Maggie's reaction and rolled his eyes. "My mother tends to overdo it on special occasions." He continued to watch Maggie's face as she looked around. He felt embarrassed to have experienced this type of extravagance his entire life while it was completely out of the ordinary for Maggie.

"This is completely amazing," Maggie exclaimed, wide-eyed.

"C'mon." Nick grabbed Maggie's hand and led her across the tent that was quickly beginning to fill. "Let me introduce you around, then we can eat something if you want and take off. Sound good?"

"That sounds perfect." Then again, anything that Nick suggested would have sounded perfect, as long as Maggie was with him. She felt closer to him with every minute that passed.

Maggie met more people that afternoon than she ever had at one time. She was introduced to friends of Samantha's, old business associates of Nick's father, acquaintances of Mrs. Winters. (Maggie still didn't feel comfortable calling her "Patricia"). She was tired after a while and Nick sensed it...he was tired of being there, as well, and was looking for the first opportunity for the two of them to make an exit. He knew, however, that if he skipped out too early his mother would let him hear about it later, so he tried to make sure he circulated enough before finally whispering in Maggie's ear.

"What do you say we get out of here now? People here are starting to drink, and it will just get wild. We can go have dinner, just the two of us. Does that sound okay?"

Maggie sighed with relief. "That's the best suggestion I've heard all day."

Nick grabbed Maggie's hand and led her through the crowd quickly; afraid to look up at anyone for fear that they would stop him to talk if he made eye contact. Once they made it out to Nick's truck, it took a bit of maneuvering to get it out of the driveway. Within minutes, however, they were headed down the road.

"Thank you so much for putting up with all of that," Nick said to Maggie as he draped his arm around her shoulders. "I know that was a lot to deal with. I'm just glad you were there with me."

Maggie kicked off her sandals, her feet hot and tired. "There's no place I would have rather been." She curled her legs under her on the seat of the truck and leaned her head on to Nick's shoulder.

"So where are we headed, anyway?" Nick took his eyes off of the road briefly to glance down into Maggie's beautiful eyes. "You said you had an idea."

Maggie suddenly felt embarrassed by her suggestion and blushed. She picked at the hem of her dress as she answered. "Oh, it was nothing, really." She paused. "I was just thinking that we could go to your cabin. My grandmother is entertaining her friends at our house tonight, and the cabin is the only place I can think of where we could be alone." She said these words quietly, softly, and kept her eyes downcast briefly before raising them to meet Nick's.

Nick felt his heart skip a beat: he had wanted to make the same suggestion, but was afraid that Maggie would get the wrong idea. He leaned over and whispered, "That sounds like a great plan."

After stopping at a local convenience store to get sodas and a few items to make sandwiches with, Nick headed in the direction of the cabin. The sun was just starting to go down, and beautiful, energetic shades of color burst across the sky. The truck window was down, and the evening air, which was turning unseasonably cool, blew in and whipped around the cab. Maggie snuggled closer to Nick, absorbing his warmth through his thin cotton shirt.

They both remained silent, feeling completely comfortable to do so. They each were lost in thought, both thinking of each other and the happiness in their hearts.

Within minutes, Nick pulled onto the dirt road where the cabin was located. After pulling up and stopping, the two got out of the truck and began to gather bags of food to carry in.

"It looks like we're planning on feeding an army," Maggie teased. "Or you must be really hungry, one of the two."

Nick smiled back at Maggie without responding. He located the key to the cabin from his key ring and unlocked the front door, then held it open for Maggie. They put the groceries away silently. Maggie thought how much she wished that things could be like this all the time: the two of them spending time together, almost as if they were a married couple. The thought surprised Maggie, considering how she had always said she would *never* be married. She sucked in her breath silently.

"You're awfully quiet." Nick's voice was warm, and Maggie looked up from the task of folding paper bags to see him staring at her, his eyes just as affectionate as his voice.

"I don't mean to be." Maggie answered slowly. "Just thinking."

"Hungry?"

Maggie thought for a moment. "Not really. A little thirsty, maybe."

"You up for a cold beer?" Nick grinned at Maggie as he reached into the refrigerator, pulled out two beers, and handed her one after popping the top. "They've been in here a long time," Nick said. "But I don't guess beer goes bad, does it?" he asked her with a grin.

Maggie took it from him, her hand touching his slightly as she did, which instantly caused her skin to tingle. "Thank you. It's been a long time since I've had a beer."

Nick opened his next, took a drink, and set the can on the counter.

SIMPLE THINGS

"There are sodas, too, if that's what you prefer."

"No, no," Maggie replied. She felt tipsy already, just from being in Nick's presence. "This is just fine."

They stood there for a few minutes, neither saying a word; then Nick broke the silence. "Do you want to sit on the back porch? It's a nice night out."

"I'd love to." Maggie followed Nick out back to the screened porch. She sat next to him on the swing. She felt nervous; for what reason she wasn't sure. She took a drink of her beer, and as she brought the can back down from her lips she felt Nick's arm fall lightly across her shoulders.

"So tell me..." Nick began. "You were asking questions about my family earlier...now what do you think of them?"

Maggie answered quickly. "Well, I didn't get much of a chance to talk to either one of them, but they both seemed really nice. I'd really like to get to know your mother better." She paused, thinking. "You're mother sure knows how to throw a party, doesn't she? I've never seen anything quite like that!"

Nick took a drink of his beer before he responded flatly. "Yes, she's definitely good at that."

Maggie decided to change the subject, sensing that talk of the party, or the extravagance of it, made Nick uncomfortable.

"Can I ask you a question?" Maggie looked up at Nick from her position on the porch swing.

Nick raised his eyebrows at her as he took a sip of his beer, indicating for her to go ahead and ask.

"What's a guy like you doing working at a place like the diner?"

The question took Nick by surprise, and he almost choked on the beer before he could swallow.

"What do you mean, 'a guy like me'?"

"Well..." Maggie started. "I had no idea what your background was. For all I knew, you were a struggling college guy who needed the money. Yet, today...I saw your home, where you come from, and..." Her voice trailed off. She shrugged her shoulders, not sure that she wanted to continue the thought.

"And what?" Nick's voice was slow and steady.

"And I can't believe that you're working at the diner with me for peanuts. I mean, I showed you how to make our homemade barbeque sauce and iced tea like that was really a big deal. I guess I'm just embarrassed that I didn't know…" Once again, her voice trailed off.

"Maggie, please don't be embarrassed." Nick ran his fingers through his hair before he continued. "If anyone should be embarrassed, it's me for not telling you. I guess I just assumed that everyone in this town knows who the Winterses are. When you didn't act like it was a big deal when you met me, I felt relief," Nick said.

"I didn't grow up in this town, remember? I try not to pay attention to local gossip, either."

"I know, and that is one of the many things that I found–*find*–so refreshing about you. I'm used to people wanting to be around me for ulterior motives. When you come from a family like mine, you find out quickly who your friends are." Pausing to take another sip of beer, Nick squeezed Maggie's hand before he continued. "I wasn't keeping anything from you, Maggie. I stopped in the diner that night just to have some time to myself, to try and decide if I wanted to spend another summer in this sleepy little town or if I wanted to head back to NC and work. But I met you, and I saw the sign in the window, and before I knew it, my decision had been made. It was that simple."

Maggie smiled. "I believe you. I just don't understand why you did it, when you could be doing so much more with your time." Maggie paused. "But I'm glad, though. You've definitely made this summer memorable."

"And it's not over yet," Nick responded quickly.

Maggie decided to switch the subject. "It's beautiful out here," Maggie noted. "I could stay out here forever."

"Well then," Nick answered. "That's exactly what we'll have to do." He massaged the back of Maggie's neck gently, then began lightly playing with strands of her hair. They rocked gently on the swing for several minutes as they stared up at the beautiful night sky.

Maggie broke the silence, finally, by asking something that had been on her mind a lot lately. "How does your mother feel about you seeing me?"

The question surprised Nick and he wondered if Maggie had picked up on any kind of vibes from his mother. He held his breath for a minute, unsure of how to respond. He drank down the last of his beer and set the can down beside him. "She hasn't really said anything at all." It was the truth...at least so far. His mother hadn't had a chance to speak to Nick since she discovered who his "mystery" girlfriend was. "Besides," Nick continued, "It wouldn't matter what *anyone* else thinks. *I* love you, and that's what matters."

The words slipped out so effortlessly. Nick hadn't even planned on what he was going to say to Maggie, but before he realized it, he had said the words he never thought he would say to anyone. But it was true, he realized. *I love her!*

Maggie whipped her head around to face him as soon as he spoke the words. She wanted to ask if she had heard correctly, but the words wouldn't form on her lips. Before she had a chance to respond in any fashion, Nick spoke the words again.

"It's true, Maggie. I can't think of anything else, day or night, except for being with you. I dream about you. I look to the future and you're always there. I love you, Maggie. And I mean that from the bottom of my heart." He rubbed his thumb across Maggie's cheek as he spoke, and a tear slipped down her face.

Maggie raised her eyes to meet Nick's. "Oh, Nick, I love you too." She threw both arms around his neck and hugged him tightly, not wanting to let go. She realized that she'd loved Nick from the moment she met him, and the awareness of this made her squeeze him even tighter.

Nick returned the embrace, his strong arms securely fastened around her waist. After several moments they pulled apart, and the realization of their love for each other seemed to have somehow changed things between them. Nick and Maggie locked eyes, and the look that passed between them conveyed all of the emotions they had been feeling for the past several weeks.

Without saying another word, Nick leaned down toward Maggie, his lips burning for her, his tongue wanting to taste her. His mouth met hers, and Maggie kissed him back feverishly, exploring the depths of his mouth with her tongue.

Maggie felt a stirring within her that she never knew existed. She arched her back slightly and leaned back on the porch swing. Her body tingled from the top to the bottom from Nick's touch. Nick's fingers slowly traced a trail from the top of her shoulder to her fingertips, then back again before his hands rested gently on the back of her neck, underneath her hair. They continued to kiss as if their life depended upon it, each melting slowly into the other. She was aware now of Nick's warm hand on her leg, and he began sliding it slowly up her thigh.

Maggie felt her breath quicken and her heart race out of control. Her cheeks felt warm; her body tingly. She ached to have Nick, to experience the thrill of first lovemaking with her first love.

Before she could continue the thought, however, Nick pulled away abruptly. Maggie opened her eyes and stared at Nick, who quickly looked away. Feeling confused, Maggie tucked her hair behind her ears and smoothed her skirt with her hand. When her breathing slowed back to its normal pace, Maggie finally felt that she could trust herself to speak.

"Nick? What is it?"

Nick thought carefully about his answer before her responded. He ran his tan fingers through his dark hair and leaned forward on the swing. "Maggie, maybe we shouldn't…" He paused, and Maggie leaned forward as well, anxious to hang on to his every word. She reached her hand out to Nick's and he grabbed it quickly and squeezed her fingers lightly.

"What is it Nick? You can tell me anything." She held her breath in anticipation of what he was about to say.

"I…I want to make love to you, Maggie. More than anything." He looked into her eyes as he said this, and just as quickly looked back down, his eyes on his feet. "And if my perceptions are right, I think that's what you want too." Nick continued without waiting for

SIMPLE THINGS

Maggie's response. "But I don't want you to think that's all I want." He looked up again and locked eyes with Maggie. "I don't want you to feel like I'm pressuring you to do anything. We can just talk, if you want. Or we can pack up and go..."

"Shhh...." Maggie silenced Nick with her finger to his lips. "Now it's my turn to talk." Maggie and Nick once again connected with a look briefly before Maggie continued.

"I've thought about nothing other than being with you since the first night we met. I want to be with you, there's nothing I want more. Please, let's stay."

Nick looked away after a few moments and sat back on the swing, locking his fingers together behind his head. He took a deep breath and exhaled slowly. "Before I met you, I wasn't sure what I wanted out of life." Nick grabbed Maggie's hands and brought one of them up to his lips, kissing it softly. "But I know now. I want to spend the rest of my life with you. I just hope you feel the same."

Maggie once again threw her arms around Nick's neck. "I do feel the same, Nick. I love you so much. I don't care what anyone says, I just want to be with you...now and forever." Maggie reached her fingers up to stroke Nick's face. "And you're right...I *do* want to make love to you. I've never been more sure about anything in my life."

Nick stood up and looked down at Maggie. He reached out both hands to her, which she accepted. He pulled her up so that she was standing in front of him and he bent down and gently kissed her on the lips. She kissed him back slowly, then she carefully parted her lips and allowed their tongues to mingle once again. Nick moved down to Maggie's neck, planting soft kisses on it as he gently caressed her shoulders.

Maggie once again felt herself growing more excited with every kiss that Nick gave her. She kissed him back with every ounce of passion she had, gently running her hands down his back as she did so. She heard soft moaning noises and was surprised to realize that they were coming from her. Nick whispered lightly in her ear.

"Maggie?" They kept kissing, neither wanting to stop.

"Yes?"

"Let's go inside." Nick stopped kissing Maggie just long enough to pick her up. She laughed lightly as he put one arm under her shoulders and the other under her knees and lifted her quickly.

"What are you doing?" Maggie laughed excitedly, and a little nervously.

"You'll see," Nick responded.

He carried her to the small country bedroom and flipped on the light after he sat Maggie on the bed, leaving her breathless and anxious for Nick's touch.

Nick left the room quickly and returned carrying three candles in holders and a book of matches. After lighting them, he turned off the overhead light. He opened one window just enough to let a breeze in. The sound of chirping crickets filled the room as he opened the window, and Maggie was in awe of just how peaceful everything was, how right everything seemed.

Nick joined Maggie on the bed, sitting beside her. She looked up at him with adoring eyes. The candlelight caused shadows to dance on both of their faces, but they could still see the love that was in each other's eyes.

Nick reached over and kissed Maggie on the cheek, then her chin, then her lips. Maggie responded immediately, kissing Nick back with even more passion than before.

Nick slid the thin straps of her dress over her shoulders, and she quickly slid herself out of her dress, leaving only a strapless slip on. She leaned back on the soft, overstuffed pillows and Nick continued to kiss her softly all over, careful to shower her entire body with equal attention.

Maggie reached up and began to undo the buttons on Nick's shirt one by one, slowly, and with great care. Her fingers longed to touch him, to feel his skin all over with her bare hands. When she reached the last button, Nick pulled his shirt off, and Maggie couldn't resist reaching up to run her hands across his muscular chest. Nick moaned softly as Maggie did this, and he began to slowly lift her slip over her head.

SIMPLE THINGS

Nick was a generous lover, kissing Maggie from head to toe and back again while she arched her back and moaned softly, enjoying every moment. She opened her eyes briefly and caught Nick looking at her as he planted soft, wet kisses on her stomach.

As their bodies joined as one, they both felt a connection to one another deep within their souls. Their eyes locked at that final moment, and Maggie felt a warm sensation spread throughout her entire body. Her body trembled beneath his as her fingers kneaded the muscles of his back gently. She kissed his neck and tasted the salty sweat that lingered upon it. Maggie moaned again as Nick whispered her name softly, his breath hot against her cheek.

They made love again several more times throughout the night, until they were both fully content and exhausted. They finally curled up together under the quilt, Nick's arms encircling Maggie and pulling her close to his body. She nestled her face in the groove of his neck and planted a warm, tender kiss before they both closed their eyes and wafted off to sleep.

Maggie awoke sometime in the early morning and immediately reached over to pat Nick's side of the bed, only to find it empty. She grabbed Nick's shirt and slipped it on, buttoning it as she walked out of the bedroom and down the small hallway. She passed a mirror on the way, and studied herself in it briefly. Her blond hair was tousled, and her skin was tanned. Any trace of make-up from the day before had vanished. She felt oddly satisfied with the look and turned away from the mirror, continuing down the hall.

The sun was just starting to come up, and the kitchen was still quite dark. Maggie looked around for Nick but didn't see him anywhere. Just when she started to check out front, she heard him call out from the back porch.

"Maggie, I'm out here."

Maggie walked out onto the porch and saw Nick sitting at the patio set sipping coffee from a mug. He smiled as she came near him, and he pulled out a chair for her.

"Sleep well?" Nick reached over and pushed Maggie's hair out of her eyes with the back of his hand.

"Too well," she responded. "What time is it?"

"A little after seven," he answered. "Would you like some coffee?"

"I'd love some." Maggie started to rise, but Nick halted her quickly.

"Make yourself comfortable while I get it." He kissed her on the cheek as he stood.

Maggie thanked him and sat back down quickly. She couldn't help but watch him as he walked past her and went into the tiny kitchen. He wore cotton drawstring pajama pants, obviously something that he had here already since neither of them had packed in advance. He was shirtless, and Maggie watched as he reached a tan arm above his head to grab a coffee mug out of the cupboard.

"Cream or sugar?" Nick asked the question with his back to her.

"Cream, please," Maggie answered back. She continued to watch him as he poured the coffee, then he turned and headed back toward her with the steaming mug in his hand.

He set it down carefully in front of her before taking his seat.

"I want to know everything about you," he said to her in a warm and honest voice. "Just *starting* with how you take your coffee." He lifted his mug to his lips and sipped.

Maggie smiled and responded quickly. "The feeling is mutual."

They sat for several contented minutes in silence, listening to the birds chirp and the rain fall lightly, something that had come on sometime during the night. Maggie felt a feeling of warmth spread throughout her body. Once again, she couldn't believe the events that had transpired over the past several weeks. It seemed like a dream that she was living; yet here she was, in a small cozy cabin in the woods, with the most wonderful man she had ever met, listening to the rain, and wearing his shirt. She almost felt like pinching herself to prove that everything was real.

These thoughts of just how content she was with life right now led other, less pleasant, thoughts into her mind. She knew, as much as she hated to think about it, that the time would come for Nick to head back to college, back to his life in North Carolina. She shuddered

SIMPLE THINGS

at the thought of him leaving. Sometimes she managed to surprise herself with just how attached she felt to Nick...after all, she had always assured herself that she would *never* be seriously involved with anyone. She had spent a lot of time alone growing up, just as she had told Nick, and had come to rely on no one but herself. And of course her grandmother, but that was completely different.

Now, her heart ached at the thought of him leaving or the thought of her being alone again. The feelings of discontent must have shown on her face, for Nick touched her lightly on the arm to draw her attention back to the present.

"Are you okay? You're frowning." Nick noticed every little detail about Maggie now. "Are you worried about explaining your night out to your grandmother?"

Maggie wished that was her only worry, and she decided to use this opportunity to tell Nick her biggest fear. Sighing, she responded slowly. "I just don't want you to leave, that's all."

"Well, we don't have to go anywhere for a while," Nick answered, not understanding the true meaning behind her words. "I told my mother that I would break the tents down today and get the chairs picked up from the party. But that can wait."

Maggie smiled at Nick's response before gently shaking her head. "That's not what I meant. I was just wondering when, exactly, you will be going back to school." Nervously, she took a deep breath and added, "How much longer will this last?"

Taken aback, Nick stood up and came around quickly to Maggie's side of the table. He knelt down in front of her and grabbed her by both wrists, gently restraining her as he stared deeply into her eyes. "What do you mean? Who says this has to end?" He let go of one wrist and pulled her chin up when she started to look away, forcing her to make eye contact.

Maggie lifted her eyes to meet his, and melted at the sight of his deep blue eyes staring back at her. She reached up and touched his cheek with the back of her hand.

"No one says." She shifted her eyes downward once again. "I guess I'm just a realist. I know that you have to go back sometime, and it's so easy to slip back into the way things were…you know, before we met."

"Hey…don't talk like that. Don't you dare," Nick said softly.

"I do want to know when you have to go, though," Maggie said sincerely. "It will be the worst day of my life, but I'd like to know now."

"Sometime in September, after Labor Day," Nick answered as he walked to the kitchen with his now empty mug. "Which means we have two months before we even have to think about that," he called over his shoulder. "So let's not."

Maggie agreed, at least for the moment, to put all thoughts of his leaving aside. "I guess I really should get home," Maggie said as she pushed back from the table and stood. "I need to help my grandma out with a few things around the house. I'm sure she's wondering what I've been up to." Maggie raised her eyebrows and gave Nick a mischievous grin as she walked toward him and wrapped her arms around his waist. Her face was buried in his chest, and his strong arms wrapped around her in return. He inhaled the sweet perfumed scent of her silky hair and planted several kisses on the top of her golden head.

"I guess we should be going, then," Nick said to her as they reluctantly broke their embrace.

They spent the next several minutes tidying up and gathering their belongings. Maggie grudgingly took off Nick's shirt in the small bathroom and dressed quickly in her outfit from the day before. She held the shirt in front of her and inhaled deeply, enjoying the lingering scent of Nick's masculine body. She folded the shirt carefully and draped it over her forearm before stepping out into the hallway.

Maggie found Nick outside, quickly packing what few items they had brought into his truck. His hair was damp from the light rain that continued to fall. Maggie watched briefly from the doorway before she ran to the passenger side of the truck, jumped in, and waited patiently for Nick to finish locking up.

They spent the ride home in silence, their minds filled with pleasant thoughts of the previous evening. When Nick pulled into

Maggie's drive, they both sat for a moment, neither saying a word. Nick turned toward Maggie and placed his hand behind her neck lightly. She smiled up at him, once again thinking to herself just how handsome he was.

"I don't want last night to change things between us," Nick said when he finally spoke. "I want this just to be the beginning of things to come."

Maggie exhaled slowly. "I feel the same way." She tucked her damp hair behind her ear and looked down at her lap. "I had a wonderful time." She looked up in time to meet his blue eyes staring down at her, and her breath was momentarily taken from her. A dark lock of hair fell across Nick's eye, and Maggie reached up slowly to touch it.

"I guess I should be going," Maggie said as she dropped her hand back into her lap.

Nick sighed. "You and me both. I have a lot to do today." He paused before adding, "But I'd rather spend the day with you."

Maggie shook her head lightly. "Do what you need to do, I understand. I need to get some things done as well."

Nick nodded in response.

He walked Maggie to the door, even though she insisted that he didn't have to. He kissed her lightly on the lips and then on the cheek. He then leaned down and whispered into Maggie's ear. "I love you."

His breath tickled and Maggie giggled softly. "I love you too, Nick."

Nick sighed heavily and turned in the direction of his truck, not wanting to leave her.

"Wait." Maggie's voice stopped Nick in his tracks and he turned slowly back around to face her.

"Won't you come back and eat dinner with us this afternoon?" Maggie's voice pleaded.

Nick sighed once more. "I wish I could, Maggie." He shook his head from side to side. "But I can't." He stuck his thumbs through the front belt loops of his pants and looked up at her beautiful face as he spoke.

Maggie tried to conceal her discontent. "Another time, then."

Nick smiled broadly, showing his dimple that Maggie found so irresistible. "You can count on it." He blew her a kiss before turning to walk to his truck. He threw his hand up in a wave as he backed out of the driveway.

Maggie stood on the porch for a few moments as she watched Nick drive away. *I am so much in love*, she thought, a smile spreading across her lips. She never knew that it was possible to feel this way about anyone. Sighing softly, Maggie stood up tall and stretched her arms above her head. She turned to head indoors, curious about what kinds of questions she would get from her grandma.

CHAPTER 9

Nick had similar thoughts as he drove across town to his mother's country estate. He hadn't had a moment alone with his mother since the graduation and he wondered if she had sat up all night waiting on him to return home. Knowing her, she probably had.

He had almost decided to stay with Maggie when he dropped her off. He wanted to be with her more than anything, but he knew he would just be putting off the inevitable–facing his mother, that is.

As Nick pulled into the driveway, the garage door was up and he noticed that his mother's car was nowhere in sight. He let out a sigh of relief...at least she wasn't waiting at the door ready to pounce.

I wouldn't care if she was, though, Nick thought as he slammed his truck door and headed up the walkway. *I love Maggie, and my mother will just have to accept it. End of story.* Then why, in the pit of his stomach, did he feel that it wasn't going to be quite that easy?

As he pushed open the front door to the house, he immediately heard his mother call out. "Back so soon?"

Her voice startled him; since her car wasn't there, he assumed that she wouldn't be either. She was standing in the kitchen, her head cocked to one side, putting an earring through her earlobe. Two packed suitcases sat at her feet. She was dressed in a smart linen pantsuit, beige with matching pumps.

"I thought you were Roger," his mother responded flatly as she finished latching the earring into place. "He took the car to get it serviced before taking us to the airport."

"Where are you off to?" Nick asked curiously.

His mother looked at him as if he were foolish. "Now what have I been talking about for the past several weeks? Your sister and I are headed to the Bahamas. Her graduation present, remember?"

Nick had completely forgotten. His mother and Samantha were

going to be gone for two weeks–the first week to the Bahamas, the second week to Pennsylvania to check out the college that his sister would be attending in the fall. Nick hadn't even been asked to go along...not that he would have. Besides, it would give him two weeks alone with Maggie.

The thought of Maggie made him smile to himself, and obviously his mother picked right up on that.

"We need to have a serious talk before I leave." Patricia spoke slowly, carefully enunciating each word. "And I think you know what it's about."

"No, I don't, Mother," Nick responded flatly. "Why don't you tell me?"

"For starters, I don't like that you are seeing that Clark girl."

"Her name is Maggie," Nick corrected.

Patricia ignored his interjection and continued. "She isn't your type, Nick. She's not *our* type."

"Since when did my personal relationships become *ours*?" Nick shot back. "You don't know a thing about Maggie, and I can tell from your attitude that you never intend to."

Patricia sighed heavily. This was going to be worse than she had originally thought.

"Just what is the nature of your relationship? I assume that it's just a passing, summer thing. But all the same, it doesn't look good, your being around her. I know a lot about her family from way back before you were born. I don't want my son associated with their kind of people." Patricia crossed her arms in front of her and stared eye to eye with Nick.

Nick felt his blood boiling. He had known all along that his mother would give him a hard time about Maggie, he just hadn't known to what lengths she would go to in trying to come between them. He willed himself to take a deep breath, to calm down, before answering. "Mother, this is not open for discussion. I enjoy spending time with Maggie. She feels the same. That's all you need to know. She's a wonderful person, if you would just *try* to get to know her."

Patricia rolled her eyes toward the ceiling. "Right," she responded sarcastically. "You would be Miss Wonderful too if you were in her shoes, a poor girl trying to woo the town's wealthiest young bachelor."

Nick gritted his teeth. The muscles in his jaw clenched tightly. "Don't you dare say that about her. Maggie didn't even know who I was when we met."

Patricia let out a high pitched laugh. "You honestly believe that? Boy, you *are* naive. Of course she knew who you were. And if she claimed not to, I know for a fact that her grandmother does. Surely she would have let her granddaughter in on *that* little secret, don't you think?"

Nick felt his face flush. He clenched and unclenched his fists along his sides. "Maggie is also not a liar. If she says she didn't know, then she didn't know."

A moment of silence elapsed before any other words were spoken. Nick felt disgusted. This should be the greatest time of his life, and his mother was ruining it with her sarcasm and negativity. *Trying* to ruin it, he should say. Nothing was going to spoil his relationship with Maggie, including his mother.

Patricia interrupted his thoughts abruptly. "I want to make something very clear, Nicholas. I don't like that you are seeing her, and even further I don't like that you brought her around *my friends* without at least giving me a warning. You know how I feel about that kind of thing. That was rude and disrespectful." She glared at him, expecting an apology but receiving none. She continued. "I also found out that you have been working at that greasy spoon that her grandmother runs over on Main Street. What do you think you're doing?! Are you trying to royally embarrass me? Or are you just doing charity work?"

Nick fired back hotly. "I work there because I want to. It's hard work, yes, but it's satisfying. That's something you would never understand."

Patricia came within inches of Nick's face. Through gritted teeth, she spat, "Believe me when I tell you that she is wrong for you. I should know my own son. And I know what kind of background she comes from. You're way out of her league. And I'd bet my last dollar that she's only attracted to you for what she can get. No one can change my mind on that." That being said, she stood and waited for a response, breathing heavily.

Nick shook his head slowly and chuckled to himself. "You never quit, do you? The sad thing is, Maggie *likes* you. She talked about how 'nice' you seemed. And you stand here and talk about her like she's nothing when you don't know a thing about her."

Patricia ignored his comment. "You have until the time I get back to fix it. Get rid of her. Or I will. And quit that job. You're making a fool out of yourself *and* me. I won't have it. I don't have to pay for your last year of college, you know."

"Is that a threat?"

"You're smart. Figure it out."

At that moment the doorbell rang. Mother and son glared at each other, neither moving a muscle. Finally, Patricia turned slowly to retrieve her bags. "Tell your sister it's time to go."

Those were the last words Patricia spoke to Nick before she left. Nick summoned Samantha and helped load her suitcases into the trunk of the sleek gold Lexus that was parked in the driveway. Roger, a middle-aged gentleman that had worked around the house for years doing odd jobs, assisted Nick with loading the bags before he climbed behind the wheel. He would be driving the two to the airport and returning the car to the house later.

Nick stood in the driveway and watched them back out. He threw his hand up in a slight wave before heading back inside.

The first thing he did after going in was head to the telephone. He dialed a number, and Maggie answered on the first ring.

"Maggie? It's Nick. I'll be there for dinner after all. What should I bring?"

Nick showed up promptly at six o'clock. He tapped lightly on the screen door. Maggie ran from the kitchen to let him in.

"It sure smells good in here," Nick said as he reached around Maggie's waist and pulled her to him. He kissed her lightly on the lips.

SIMPLE THINGS

Maggie nervously looked around the corner to see if her grandmother was in sight. She giggled and kissed him back quickly. "You've never had my grandmother's fried chicken. You're in for a real treat."

Nick followed her into the kitchen where various pots were steaming on the stove. He handed Lily a bottle of sparkling grape juice that he had picked up on the way over.

"I told you not to bring anything!" Lily chided. "What's this?"

"Nothing much," Nick replied. "It's the least I could do for a home cooked meal. Don't you get tired of doing so much cooking?"

"I never get tired of cooking as long as people enjoy it," Lily responded sincerely. "Maggie, you two grab something cold to drink and sit out on the porch if you like. Dinner will be ready shortly."

Maggie poured them each a glass of lemonade and led Nick out to the front porch. Although the day had been quite warm, the afternoon was cooling off nicely. The two of them sat on the swing pre-occupied with their own thoughts for several minutes. A squirrel scampered across the front lawn in search of food. A dog howled in the distance.

Nick's mind still whirled with the conversation that had taken place earlier between him and his mother. She had actually threatened him! Although it was a *weak* threat. He knew it and she knew it. He had an inheritance coming to him because of his father's death that he was set to receive when he turned twenty-two. *Less than a year away*. If worse came to worse, he could take out a loan through the school to pay for his last year.

And even if he couldn't, that was fine too. He could go back to school later, after he received his inheritance. But no matter what obstacle his mother would try to throw at him, he would manage. He just knew that no one, his mother included, was going to keep him from being with Maggie.

"You're awfully quiet," Maggie noted. "What's on your mind?"

Nick shrugged. "This and that. What did Lily say when you got here this morning?"

"Actually, she wasn't here."

"But her truck was." Nick took a gulp of lemonade, enjoying the tart taste as he swallowed.

"I know. A lady from church picked her up early. They had some kind of meeting. Anyway, she assumed I came in late last night and was still sleeping when she left."

"And you didn't correct her, I take it?"

Maggie blushed sheepishly and shook her head. "No, I didn't. I can talk about some things with my grandmother, but others...well, I'd rather keep them to myself."

Nick smiled at her. "I know what you mean."

They lapsed into comfortable silence once again. Nick put his arm around Maggie and she slid a little closer to him on the swing. Within minutes, they heard Lily yell that dinner was ready. Nick stood and held out his hand for Maggie, pulling her up quickly. Hand in hand, they went inside to join Lily at the table.

Everyone agreed that dinner was delicious. The menu consisted of fried chicken, mashed potatoes and gravy, lima beans, corn on the cob, and homemade biscuits. Dessert was peach pie a la mode.

Nick thanked Lily over and over for inviting him. "I can't remember the last time I ate this good."

Lily laughed it off with a wave of her hand. "It was my pleasure. You're welcome here anytime, Nick," she said, meaning every word.

Nick thought about those words as everyone finished up dessert. Lily had extended an open invitation to him in her home, yet his own mother wouldn't give Maggie the time of day. He really resented his mother's attitude. Having money might be a nice amenity in life, but it didn't mean that you were above others. He shook his head slightly as he recalled once again their conversation from earlier. His mother would never change. Of that he was certain.

Nick finished up his pie and wiped his mouth with a cloth napkin. He made a silent vow to forget the words his mother had said. The time was counting down until he would have to leave and go back to college, something that he didn't want to think about right now. He wanted to do nothing more than enjoy these next couple of months with Maggie. That was all he planned on doing.

CHAPTER 10

Maggie and Nick spent almost every waking hour together over the next two weeks. The diner stayed packed from morning until evening. Although tired when they left, Maggie and Nick always spent time together in the evening hours as well. They went to the cabin the following Saturday evening and made love under the stars on the quilt that Nick removed from the bed.

Another night they went dancing in nearby Chesterfield. Nick held Maggie close as they two-stepped across the dusty wooden floor of a smoke filled room, all eyes in the bar on them. She couldn't help but feel proud as she watched other girls eyeing him, as she was the one by his side.

Maggie cherished every moment that she spent with him. She felt herself growing closer to Nick with every passing moment.

Nick felt the same about Maggie. When he dropped her off at her grandmother's each evening, he would go home and lay awake for hours, thinking about when he would see her again and how he would pass the time until then. He tried to make each evening more special than the next. He sent flowers to her home, took her to dine in nice restaurants, and took her to see movies at the local theater. Other evenings they would choose to sit on the porch and watch the stars, talking about their future.

On the Saturday evening before Nick's mother was due to return home, Nick insisted on having Maggie over for dinner. After the diner closed, Maggie headed home with her grandmother. She showered quickly and toweled off, then dressed in a short blue-jean sun dress and a pair of sandals. She pulled her blond tresses back into a low ponytail and wore the pearl necklace and earrings that she had worn on their first date.

She borrowed her grandmother's truck and drove over to Nick's house. The house was overly large and impressive, almost eery in the dark. Moonlight caused shadows to be cast along the walkway. Before she could ring the doorbell, the door opened quickly. Maggie's heart flip-flopped in her chest. Nick was wearing faded blue jeans with holes torn at each knee. He had on a white tee shirt and a red baseball cap turned backwards.

Nick held the door open wide and motioned for Maggie to come in. "After you, madam." He said this with a fake accent and took a slight bow as she walked through the threshold, and Maggie couldn't help but laugh.

"Why thank you, sir," Maggie replied. She kicked her sandals off at the door. "I hope you don't mind," she said to Nick as she did so. "But I noticed that you aren't wearing shoes, so I might as well join you."

Maggie followed Nick into the kitchen, looking around as she walked. The house was beautiful and contemporary, not her style, and almost had a sterile feel to it. Nick caught her looking at a nude ivory carving of a man and woman in the dining room.

"My mom's taste, not mine," he said with a shrug. "But what can I do? I just live here every now and then." He gave her a smile, trying to help her relax.

"Do you mind if I look around the rest of the house?" Maggie asked. "I only saw the downstairs portion the day of your sister's graduation party."

Nick wiped his hands on a tea towel. "Sure, let's go. I'll give you the guided tour."

They walked from room to room, Nick pointing out what various paintings and sculptures were and where they had come from. Maggie listened with interest and asked various questions.

"When do I get to see your room?" Maggie asked with a smile as she batted her eyelashes.

"Why, Miss Clark, if that's what you wanted to see, why didn't you say so? We would have gone there first," Nick teased back. He grabbed her hand and led her to the end of the hall. He pushed open a large oak door and flipped on a light switch.

SIMPLE THINGS

Maggie took her time looking around the room at various photo frames. She saw Nick in photos with friends, apparently from college. In one she noticed a beautiful redhead with full, red lips sitting on Nick's lap planting a kiss on his cheek. "Who's this?" Maggie asked curiously. "Old girlfriend?"

Nick walked over to peer at the picture himself. "Her? Nah." He shook his head. "Her name is Natalie Mason. Her father and mine were close friends, old roommates from college. Her dad is some kind of investment banker." Nick shrugged. "I've known her for years. Strictly platonic." He paused. "At least on my end."

"She sure looks like she's having a good time," Maggie noted. "Can't say that I blame her, sitting on such a good looking guy's lap." Maggie tickled Nick in the ribs. "Just make sure she knows that you belong to me, now, and we won't have a problem," Maggie teased.

Nick pulled Maggie down on the bed by her wrist. "Do I detect a little jealousy?" Nick kissed Maggie on the neck and pinned her arms playfully above her head. "It's always nice to be a wanted man."

Maggie giggled and responded by kissing Nick back. Nick's hand slowly slid up the back of her leg as they kissed, finally coming to rest on the back of her thigh. Their breath quickened and their hearts raced. Finally, Maggie grudgingly pushed Nick off and tried to sit up. "I thought you brought me here for dinner," she teased. "Was this all a ploy to get me into your bedroom?" Her tone was flirtatious, and Nick responded in kind.

"Well, now that you mention it…"

Maggie laughed. Her tone then turned serious. "You make me so happy, Nick. Just in case I haven't told you that lately, I thought you'd like to know." She reached up and stroked the side of his face gently.

"You have, but it's always nice to hear. I love you, Maggie."

"I love you too."

Nick reluctantly pushed himself up off of the bed. He extended a hand to Maggie and pulled her to her feet in one swift motion. "I promised you dinner, and that's what you're going to get. Have you had enough of the tour?"

Although Nick didn't want Maggie to help with dinner, she had a hard time sitting still and watching. She chopped vegetables for the salad while Nick grilled steaks on the patio. "I marinated these steaks overnight," Nick said. "My own secret recipe."

Impressed, Maggie responded, "And where did you learn to do that?"

"I cooked a lot for myself and Samantha when we were growing up. I used to experiment with different recipes, and the marinade is one of my favorites."

"What's in it?" Maggie asked curiously.

"If I told you that, it wouldn't be a secret," Nick said with a teasing wink as he walked through the French doors onto the patio to check the progress of the steaks.

Maggie laughed and tossed a tea towel at him, missing him completely. "Real funny."

They ate dinner outside on the patio, with no other noise other than the chirping of crickets and their own conversation. Maggie took a bite of her steak and closed her eyes in enjoyment. "Nick, this is wonderful. You can grill steak for me any day."

"And I will," he responded. "Gladly."

They ate in silence for a while as they both enjoyed their meal. Maggie decided to bring up a new subject. "Tell me about your father." She took a drink of tea and waited for Nick's response.

He finished chewing a bite of steak and bit his lower lip. "My father. There's so much I could tell. What would you like to know?" He sat back in his chair and studied Maggie closely. "Anything in particular?"

Maggie shook her head and shrugged her shoulders lightly. "Anything you're willing to share."

Nick tilted his head back and stared up at the night sky. The moon was full, and it cast a bright yellow glow across the patio. The stars were plentiful and bright. A chorus of cicadas sang a harmonious tune in the distance.

Nick, obviously deep in thought, responded slowly. "We were

very close," he began. "He was a great person. He was honest and fair, in everything he did." Nick smiled softly as he remembered. "I remember that I never got punished without an explanation as to why, or without being told 'This will hurt me more than it will hurt you'." Nick paused to take a drink of his tea before he continued. "My mother grew up with sisters and always claimed that she 'didn't know what to do with a boy.' So, partly because of that, I spent the majority of my time with my father. He traveled several times a year with his practice, and as I got older, I was allowed to go along. I thought I was something, hanging out at important meetings with official looking people." Nick laughed again.

Maggie watched him intently, hanging on to his every word.

Nick continued. "My mother was never into the nature scene, I think I told you that before. Afraid that she would break a fingernail, I guess." Nick laughed and Maggie did also. "No, really, it just never was her thing. The cabin my dad bought was mostly for the two of us to get away. He taught me how to fish, to hunt, to do just about anything in the outdoors. I learned a lot from him. And I miss him everyday."

Maggie watched as Nick spoke, a far off look in his eyes. She reached across the table and placed her hand on top of Nick's. "I wish I could have met him."

Nick brought his thoughts back to the present and fixed his gaze on Maggie. "He would have loved you," he said. And he would have, Nick knew that for a fact.

"I wonder what brought the two of them together," Maggie pondered out loud.

"My parents, you mean?"

Maggie drew in a deep breath. "Yeah...don't you wonder? I mean, if they were that different, it makes you question their reasons for getting married."

"I've thought about that a lot, believe me," Nick responded. "I know they say opposites attract, but..." His voice trailed off.

Maggie smiled at him and shrugged. "Well, for whatever reason, I'm glad they got together."

"Are you?" Nick asked as he lifted his eyebrows at Maggie. "Why?"

"Because if they didn't, you wouldn't be alive today," Maggie said back softly. "I don't even want to think about that."

Nick smiled at her and stood up. He walked around to her side of the table and pulled out her chair. He held out his hand and winked down at her. "May I have this dance?"

Maggie giggled and placed her dainty hand in Nick's masculine one. Standing, she replied, "Why, I'd be honored. But there's no music," she whispered as Nick pulled her body close to his.

Nick began a slow dance with Maggie. He placed his hands on her waist as hers slid carefully around the back of his neck. "We'll make our own music," he whispered into her ear.

Maggie's body melted into Nick's as they began to move in sync with one another. She placed her head on Nick's chest and closed her eyes. Oh, how she wished she could stay like this forever! She could think of nothing she'd like more than to spend every day of her life waking up with Nick.

"Want to go upstairs?" Nick interrupted her thoughts.

"I should help you clean the kitchen," Maggie answered.

"Do I look like I'm worried about cleaning up? I've got plenty of time for that in the morning." Nick grabbed her hand and nodded toward the house. "C'mon."

Maggie laughed and tried to protest. "Nick, I can't stay..." She lowered her voice to a mere whisper. "But you're making it so hard to say no." She playfully allowed herself to be pulled forward.

"I knew you couldn't resist," Nick whispered.

The two of them crawled across Nick's bed once they got upstairs. All they did for the next two hours was merely talk, about anything and everything. Nick told Maggie how he felt the first time he saw her. "You took my breath away," he said. "Without a doubt."

"I was so captivated by you that I didn't trust myself to speak," Maggie shared. "That was the best thing you've ever done, coming into the diner, you know." Maggie leaned over and planted a kiss on Nick's lips. She scooted closer to him and rested her head on his

SIMPLE THINGS

arm. Nick squeezed her tight.

"I know. Believe me, I know."

Maggie felt so comfortable and safe wrapped in Nick's arms. She didn't want to move, although she knew she needed to get home. She had gotten by with it last time by staying out with Nick all night; she couldn't risk doing it again. She doubted that her grandmother would say much about it, but she didn't want to give the wrong impression. To anyone. Surely, though, being with Nick couldn't be wrong. It felt too right. But still…she didn't want her grandmother thinking that she was going down the wrong path. Her grandmother had already been through a lot, and Maggie didn't want to give her any reason to worry.

Maggie wanted to get home before it got too late, crawl into her bed, and dream all night long of being with Nick forever. But being here, being by Nick's side, made it so difficult to make such a decision. Maggie looked down at his now sleeping face. His breathing was rhythmical and peaceful. She kissed him on the cheek and nudged him gently.

"Nick?" she whispered softly.

He responded with a low groan, obviously in a deep sleep already. Reluctantly, Maggie sat up and fumbled in his bed stand drawer for a pen and paper. She wrote a quick note to explain her departure and kissed him once again before heading downstairs.

Slipping her sandals on by the front door, Maggie removed her purse from the coat tree where she had placed it earlier. She eased the door open gingerly and stepped out into the silent night. An owl hooted in the distance. Her heels clicked on the smooth sidewalk. Before she reached the drivers side door, she saw headlights approaching. Maggie froze in her tracks. *Who could be coming here this time of night?* She checked her watch quickly. One twenty seven a.m. The car approached slowly and pulled in to the driveway next to Lily's truck. Maggie stood in the same spot, unable to make her feet go forward. Surely, it couldn't be Mrs. Winters. Didn't Nick say that she was coming home tomorrow?

Maggie watched as the back passenger door was flung open.

Patricia Winters, dressed impeccably, alighted from the car and stared at her. Maggie felt very uncomfortable. *This is not going to look good,* she mused to herself. *Especially with Nick upstairs sleeping. This is just what I wanted to avoid.* Maggie wished desperately that she had left just a few minutes earlier; then this entire situation would have been avoided. Oh well, there was nothing she could do about that now. Smiling and pulling all of her courage together, Maggie called out. "Did you have a nice trip?"

Patricia Winters walked slowly toward Maggie as Samantha climbed out of the car and Roger worked quickly to unload the luggage from the trunk. She carefully removed a pair of designer sunglasses that were perched on the top of her head. Placing the earpiece of one in the corner of her mouth, she responded. "Why, yes I did, thank you for asking." She nodded toward the house. "Where's Nicholas?"

Maggie felt her cheeks grow warm with embarrassment. "I...we...he made dinner for me. I'm afraid we've left a bit of a mess in the kitchen." Maggie stalled, realizing that she was avoiding the question. "I needed to get home, and Nick was really tired. He headed up to bed." Maggie shrugged her shoulders, hoping that it sounded plausible.

"I see," Patricia answered in a slow drawl. "And he didn't offer to walk you out? How un-chivalrous of him."

Maggie shrugged once again. "It's no big deal, really, Mrs. Winters." She shifted her weight to the other foot and asked, "Did you decide to come back early?"

Patricia asked with a small smile, "Surely I didn't ruin your plans?"

"Plans?" Maggie gulped nervously. "No, ma'am, you didn't ruin anything. I just thought that Nick said...," Her voice trailed off. She wasn't sure where this conversation was going, and definitely didn't like the feeling it gave her one bit.

"Anyway," Patricia said, "I'm really not surprised to see you here so late. Nick does this sort of thing often, you know...entertaining beautiful women at all hours." She hoped to cause a reaction with

Maggie, and it worked.

Maggie was visibly upset by the comment, yet she tried to smile. She felt uneasy standing in the driveway with Mrs. Winters at such a late hour. Or early, depending on how you looked at it. The two maintained eye contact for several moments. Finally, Maggie spoke up, anxious to get home. "I really do need to be going. It was nice seeing you again, Mrs. Winters."

Patricia nodded a farewell as Maggie walked quickly toward the truck and climbed in. She started it and expeditiously backed out of the driveway, her heart still pounding from the encounter.

Patricia couldn't sleep. *What was that little tramp doing in my house this time of night?* It had been a long flight and a long drive home from the airport...she was tired, and the last thing she expected to see was that girl sneaking out of her house like a thief in the night.

After she had put her things away, she took a lingering bath, trying to soak away the stress of the situation she was in. Should she just let him see this girl and let it drop? No, of course not. How humiliating this was. It was unspoken knowledge that everyone knew of her past history with Ray...she felt betrayed that her own son would be involved with this girl. Maybe the girl's mother had put her up to this...one more way to get to Patricia, by going through her son. She wouldn't put anything past Claudia Clark, even after all these years.

She slipped into a satin robe after toweling off and poured a scotch from the bar she kept in the corner of her tastefully decorated bedroom. She stretched out on an ivory chaise and crossed her legs at the ankles. She gulped quickly at the strong liquid, shuddering slightly as it burned her throat. She willed herself to think quickly of a solution as she rubbed her temples with her eyes closed, the tumbler of scotch held between her thumb and forefinger of her right hand.

Maybe she should take a different approach. She didn't want her son to end up with this girl, of that much she was sure. The horror it would be if he married her...Claudia would probably get a big laugh out of it. The thought of seeing Claudia, of her becoming a part of her family albeit by marriage, reaffirmed her decision to thwart the romance between Nick and Maggie. It just wasn't meant to be, and she had to see to it that it ended. The question was how to do it without driving the two of them even closer together.

She lifted from the chaise, walked to the bar, and poured herself another. As she sat the crystal decanter back down, the plan came to her immediately. She smiled to herself as the details began to seep into her mind. Why hadn't she thought of this earlier? It could work...couldn't it? It most assuredly could, she instantly decided. She just had to be careful and calculated. One mistake on her part, and she could be exposed.

She tossed down the last of the beverage and placed the tumbler on the bar. She had to change her tactic too, until she could arrange everything. Appear accepting about this girl, but not overly so. If the change seemed too radical, Nick would surely know that something was up her sleeve.

Having made the decision, Patricia climbed in to bed and turned off the lamp on her bed stand. She had a phone call that she needed to make first thing in the morning. Once that was done, she would just sit back and wait until everything fell into place.

CHAPTER 11

Nick was surprised to wake up at six o'clock in the morning and find the other side of the bed empty. He was disappointed, but knew that Maggie wouldn't have felt comfortable sleeping there. He had to respect her for that. He had been so tired; he didn't even remember her leaving. He turned on his bedside lamp and rubbed his eyes. He immediately saw a folded piece of paper propped up against the lamp with his name on it in pretty feminine handwriting. He sat up and reached for it. He began to smile as he read the words.

Nick,
I'm sorry to sneak out on you, but I needed to get home. What kind of impression would I give if my truck stayed in your driveway overnight...we'd really have everyone talking! Anyway, I had a wonderful evening with you. The dinner was delicious...you are an incredible cook and an incredible host. Well, you're incredible at everything. I kissed you good-bye, but you didn't budge. I hope to hear from you soon. Until then, I will be dreaming of you...
Love,
Maggie

Nick folded the note and placed it in the top drawer of his bed stand. He got up and stretched, then peeked out his bedroom window that overlooked the backyard. It was just starting to get light out, a gray and orange tinge filling the sky. Feeling especially contented, he decided that it was a good morning to go for a jog. In fact, he might as well go and get Maggie and see if she wanted to go along. He took a quick shower and got dressed in a tee shirt and shorts. He ran down the stairs two at a time and grabbed his keys from the kitchen counter where he had left them the afternoon before. He wondered to himself what time his mother would be getting home. He shuddered at the thought. Their last meeting had not been pleasant, and he was not at all looking forward to her return.

Maggie was already up when Nick arrived. She hadn't slept well the night before. Her thoughts went back and forth between the evening with Nick and the conversation that she had had with his mother as she was leaving. She had never had to deal with a situation like this, since Nick was her first true boyfriend. She felt a little intimidated in Mrs. Winters' presence, but she hoped that she could grow closer to her and become her friend. Would that ever be possible?

Maggie was glad that Nick suggested going for a run. Since they had been together, she hadn't exercised regularly, only because she enjoyed spending her free time with Nick. After a lengthy stretch to warm up, they started off in a slow jog. They didn't talk much; both were concentrating on pacing their breathing. They jogged down old country roads that Maggie hadn't been down in quite a while. They looped around the Clines' farm and came back up past the small school complex, where the elementary, middle, and high schools were all situated together. After approximately five miles, Maggie stopped and started walking, trying to slow her breathing down. Nick jogged backwards in place while he waited for her to catch up.

"What's the matter? Can't go any further?"

Maggie stopped and shook her head. She bent over and put her hands on her hips. "No, I can't." She blew out a deep breath of air. "I guess that's what I get for not running for so long. I used to be able to run ten miles easily." She shook her head again. "But not today."

Nick stopped as well and tossed Maggie a small towel that he had brought along.

"Thanks," she replied as she took it and wiped the sweat from her brow.

They walked the remaining mile or so back to Maggie's house and their breathing reverted to normal. Maggie always felt good after she ran and she chided herself silently for putting it off for this long. "I got your note." Nick interrupted her thoughts. "It was nice, but I would have rather woken up with you there instead." He winked at her and tickled her in the ribs.

Maggie giggled and jumped to the side. "Well you *know* that I didn't want to leave," she said. "But it's a good thing I did, otherwise your mother might have caught me *in* your bedroom."

Nick stopped in his tracks. He turned toward Maggie and grabbed her gently by the elbow. "What did you say?"

Maggie's eyes widened slightly; she was unsure if she had said the wrong thing. "Umm...your mother came home as I was leaving." She said the words slowly. "Didn't you see her this morning? No, I guess she would've still been in bed. She seemed really tired...it was almost two in the morning when I talked to her."

"She wasn't supposed to come home until today. What did she say to you?" Nick's eyes probed Maggie's for information.

Maggie wasn't sure that she wanted to go into the whole conversation, especially the comment about him entertaining women, so she gave him the highlights. "I ran in to her in the driveway. I told her you had gone to bed because you were tired, and that I had to get home. That's about it."

Nick stroked his chin as he listened. Could it be that his mother was accepting his relationship after all? Surely if she had been that upset about it, she would have stormed straight to his room and descended her wrath upon him right then. That had happened many times before, especially when his mother felt that she wasn't being obeyed.

"So that's it?" Nick tried to obtain all of the details that he could.

"What is this, an interrogation?" Maggie punched him lightly in the arm. "It was no big deal. I told her that you had cooked dinner for me; I asked her about her trip. Anyway, didn't you see her car in the garage this morning?"

Nick shook his head. "Either I was still so out of it when I left that I didn't notice, or Roger drove it home to detail it for her. She's very particular about her car, among other things."

"Roger...is he the older guy that was driving?"

Nick nodded. "He's worked for my parents for years."

They walked a little further in silence. The sun was out and shining brightly, all clouds from earlier had dissipated.

Nick began to rub his arm, feigning soreness. "You sure pack a mean punch."

Maggie laughed. "I didn't hit you that hard. Do you want me to?" She teased him.

"Sure, just not with your fist," Nick joked back as he reached for her hand.

Maggie invited Nick in when they arrived at her house, but he declined, anxious to get home and shower. "I'd better talk with my mother since I haven't seen her in so long. And I need to clean up that kitchen too. Maybe I can get to that mess before she sees it," he said.

"Oh, that's right. I forgot about that. Give me a few minutes and I can go along to help."

Nick shook his head. "No, no, I couldn't ask you to do that. Besides, I have a few things I need to get done. But I'll call you later, okay?" Before waiting for a reply, Nick kissed Maggie quickly on the lips and jogged to his truck. He didn't see her as she waved goodbye. His eyes were strictly glued to the road in front of him.

When he arrived home, he found that the kitchen had already been cleaned. Feeling guilty, he looked around the house for any trace of his mother. He found her out on a chaise lounge by the pool, an oversized hat shielding the sun from her eyes. She was reading a magazine and placed it to the side when she saw Nick approaching.

"Sorry about the mess in the kitchen," he stammered. "You're back early."

"Rosie was here earlier to clean. But I would appreciate it if you wouldn't leave it filthy like that again." She paused to take a sip of tea from a large glass. "And yes, I am back early. We saw everything we needed to see and your sister was anxious to get back to see her friends. Frankly, I was ready to get back myself." She patted the end of a chaise that was situated next to her, indicating that she wanted

SIMPLE THINGS

Nick to sit down.

He did as she wished. He crossed his arms and then uncrossed them. He had never been able to communicate freely with his mother and now felt at a loss for words. He wanted to ask her about last night, about her running in to Maggie in the driveway. Should he mention it? Pretend that he didn't know anything and let her bring it up? He hoped desperately that his mother felt differently about his seeing Maggie after a vacation. Perhaps she had had time to think about it and realized that Maggie was the sweet girl that he had tried to explain that she was.

As if reading his mind, Patricia interrupted his thoughts. "I saw that girl leaving when I got home. Don't you remember the conversation we had before I left?"

Nick sucked in his breath. *Here we go again.* He opened his mouth to speak and then closed it quickly; unsure of what he wanted to say.

Patricia filled the silence by speaking again. "Well, I suppose it won't be long before your relationship with her is over, anyway." She took another long sip of tea through a thin straw with ruby colored lips. "Girls like her can't handle long distance relationships. She'll set her sights on someone else once you head back to college, I'm sure," she said this nonchalantly with a flip of her hand.

Nick closed his eyes and let out a breath slowly. He opened them and looked at her, feeling like he didn't know her at all. "I'm sure that's *not* the way it will be, Mother. But you can think whatever you like."

He stood then, hoping that the conversation was over. "I'm going in to shower. Did you need me to do anything for you today?"

Patricia craned her neck to look up at her son. "Just promise me that you won't bring her around here," she said brusquely. "Don't disrespect me any more than you already have."

Nick walked away without responding.

Patricia remained outside for another hour or so, soaking up rays of beautiful sunshine and considering the conversation that had just taken place. She was pleased with how she had handled the situation.

She wasn't overly offensive, yet she didn't completely accept the arrangement. Surely she hadn't given Nick any reason to question her.

She reached to a small stand for the cordless phone that she had brought out with her earlier. She had made her phone call first thing that morning, but there was no answer and she hadn't bothered to leave a message. Something of this magnitude was better discussed face-to-face, if possible.

She punched the numbers from memory with a long red fingernail. The line rang once, then twice. Just as she was about to give up for a second time, the extension was picked up and a curt "Yes?" was spoken from the other end.

Patricia cleared her throat briefly before speaking. "Natalie? Surely I didn't wake you?" she purred the question.

"Actually, you did, but that's okay," came the voice from the other end of the line. "I didn't expect to hear from you. It's been quite a while."

"Yes it has," Patricia drawled. "Too long, in fact." After a slight pause, "Listen, darling, I'm going to cut right to the chase. There is a situation here that's developed. It involves Nicholas and a young girl he's seeing."

There was silence on the other end of the line.

"I wouldn't be calling you if it wasn't important. I need your help in straightening this matter out. Would it be possible to meet for lunch?" Patricia held her breath, although she was sure of what the answer would be. After a moment, Natalie responded.

"Name the time and place. I'll be there."

Patricia pulled into the parking lot of Oliver's, a popular but quiet deli located a half hour from her home. She arrived fifteen minutes before the one o'clock scheduled time. Stepping out of the car into the humid but breezy weather, she smoothed her skirt and placed her designer handbag onto her shoulder. She obtained a table for two in a dark secluded corner, ensuring that she gave Natalie's name and description so that they would seat her promptly when she arrived.

SIMPLE THINGS

She ordered a glass of white zinfandel and waited patiently. *This has to work. If anyone can help me, Natalie can.* Natalie was the daughter of Jim Mason, a good friend of her late husband Michael. He was an investment banker from Atlanta, and a good one at that. He had handled all of Patricia's business and financial matters for years.

Natalie had always had a thing for Nick, although he had never reciprocated her feelings. He saw her in a platonic way, nothing more. Patricia had always wanted to see the two of them together. It would please her like nothing else would to have Natalie as her daughter-in-law. After all, she was a girl after Patricia's own heart. She was beautiful, bold, and daring. Her father was just as wealthy, if not more so, than Patricia herself was. Of course she wouldn't be concerned about Natalie's motives.

At that moment she saw Natalie coming toward the table. Dressed in a plain black sun dress that came to mid-thigh and black sandals, her skin lightly tanned, Patricia couldn't help but think how striking her appearance was. Her bright auburn hair was twisted into a loose up-do. She slid gracefully into the chair across from Patricia and dropped her purse into the chair next to her.

"Sorry I'm late," she said. "But I had an appointment to get my nails done." She held both hands out for emphasis. "What do you think?" She wiggled all of her fingers simultaneously.

Patricia smiled. "They're beautiful, darling." Patricia signaled to the waiter. "So tell me…how have you been? How is your father?"

Natalie talked for several minutes, updating Patricia on the latest events going on in her life. "Dad has been busy, as usual. He's working on some deal with a computer company, so I don't see much of him." She paused to take a sip of ice water that had been placed in front of her. "I'm dying to know," Natalie said as she sat her glass back down. "What is this all about?"

Patricia got down to business, filling Natalie in on what she knew about Maggie and her relationship with Nick.

Natalie listened with concentration. "Well, where do I come in?" She said this with a smirk and her eyebrows raised, knowing before

Patricia spoke of what her role would be.

Patricia discussed a few things that she had in mind. "Do you think you can handle this?"

Natalie smiled and rubbed her hands together briskly, anxious to get started. "Do you have to ask? Just tell me when."

Patricia frowned slightly. "That's what I've been trying to decide. I'll arrange the dinner at my house...your father will be invited as well, of course." She drank the last of her wine and set the glass back down. "I'll be in touch to let you know when."

Natalie smiled back at Patricia. "I can hardly wait."

CHAPTER 12

The next week or so went by smoothly. Maggie and Nick continued to see each other, although Nick made sure not to bring Maggie to his home. Maggie didn't ask about it either, only because she enjoyed being alone with him, anyway. She knew that the time was drawing closer and closer until he would be leaving, and she couldn't bear to think about it. Nor could she bear to share what precious time they had left with anyone else.

They spent several lazy afternoons at the cabin, which they had dubbed "our place." One particular afternoon, they picked up take-out and ate under the same massive oak tree that they had first eaten under all those weeks ago. After they ate, they both stretched out and talked. For the first time in quite awhile, Nick brought up the subject of his leaving.

"You know I only have a week and a half left." It was a statement, not a question. His voice was quiet and soft. He leaned back on his side, elbow bent, with his head resting on the palm of his hand.

Maggie traced circles in a small spot of dirt that was at the edge of the blanket. Without looking up, she responded. "I know. I've been trying so hard not to think about it. But the harder I try not to, the more I find myself focusing on it."

Nick nodded. "I know what you mean." After a few minutes of silence, Nick changed the subject to something more favorable. "Why don't we make big plans for next weekend? After all, your grandmother will be away. Why don't we spend the weekend in Atlanta, just the two of us?"

Maggie thought about it. Her grandmother was going on a bus with a friend of hers down to Savannah to visit her sister Ruth. She usually went once a year, closing the diner for a couple of days, just enough to have an extended weekend. Occasionally Maggie would go along, enjoying time alone shopping and walking the boardwalk while Lily and Ruth caught up on conversation. Lily had asked her to go along this year, even though she knew that Maggie would gracefully decline.

It *would* be fun to go to Atlanta with Nick. She hadn't been there for quite a while. They could shop, have dinner, stay overnight...it definitely was tempting. She sighed lazily and began picking at a blade of grass.

"Oh, I don't know, Nick. I don't think you should spend your last weekend here out of town. I'm sure your mother would rather you spend time with her before you go back. Maybe we could all go out to dinner together, or just have a nice barbeque and pool party at your house?" As much as she wanted to spend the final weekend with Nick alone, she didn't want to get on Mrs. Winters' bad side by being selfish. When Nick didn't reply, she asked again. "What do you think?"

Nick shook his head. "Maggie, I *want* to take you out of town, to show you a good time." He paused for a few minutes to let her reflect on what he had said. "Will you please go with me?" He sat up on the blanket while he waited for her response.

Maggie looked up at him and smiled. The sun was just going down behind him, the still bright rays shining like a pot of gold, illuminating his face. "As long as you're sure that's what you want. I'd love to. I think it would be fun." She sat up, too, and Nick leaned over and kissed her.

"Good, then it's settled."

Over the next few days, Maggie and Nick planned their trip with enthusiasm. They kept it to themselves, though...it would promise to be a special time for them, and they didn't want to share it with anyone else. When Lily asked Maggie what her plans were for the weekend, Maggie just shrugged and responded honestly. "I'm sure I'll find plenty to keep me busy."

Patricia, on the other hand, was in turmoil over how and when to carry her plan out. It had to be soon...otherwise Nick would return

SIMPLE THINGS

to college on good terms with Maggie, and they might continue their relationship. It *could* eventually fall apart on its own, she knew, especially with the distance involved. But she could not, *would not*, take that chance. This was something that had to end swiftly and abruptly.

Late one evening, just as she was preparing to go up to bed, she heard the phone ringing. Sighing, she turned to walk toward it in disgust, wondering who could be calling at this time of night.

She put the receiver to her ear quickly, but just as she tried to form the word "hello" on her lips, her breath caught and she didn't say anything. She heard Nick talking and realized that it was Maggie who had called...Nick obviously was quicker to the draw than she was in answering. She couldn't help herself from listening, and she didn't feel guilty about it either. She needed to know what was going on in Nick's life–and if he didn't tell her, then how else was she supposed to find anything out?

She slowly and quietly dropped into a chair in the breakfast nook and listened, her back rigid in an uncomfortable position. She was afraid to shift in the chair for fear of making too much noise.

"I miss you." The voice was low and purring.

"I miss you too," Nick responded. "But we'll see each other first thing in the morning. Can you handle waiting until then?" Patricia could hear the smile in his voice.

"Not really," Maggie responded. "But I guess I have no choice." There was silence briefly. Patricia held her breath, afraid that she would be caught eavesdropping. "I can't wait until this weekend." Patricia's ears perked up. *This weekend?*

"I know," Nick said. "We'll have a great time."

"When do you want to leave?"

"Maybe Saturday morning," Nick answered. "Does that sound okay?"

They continued their conversation for several more minutes, Patricia learning more and more details about their planned getaway. She had to act, and quickly. She realized now that she had been waiting for an occasion like this to put her plan into action.

After Maggie and Nick said their good-byes, Patricia slowly and carefully replaced the receiver. She glanced at the grandfather clock in the foyer. Just before eleven. She tapped a long nail on the counter, her mind whirling about what she should do. It was late, but this couldn't wait. She picked up the phone once again and quickly dialed Natalie's number.

CHAPTER 13

Nick got ready for work the next morning and ran downstairs to grab some juice from the refrigerator. He flipped on the light and was startled to see his mother sitting out on the patio. It was just starting to get light, but he could see her figure at the table, a cigarette lit in her right hand. Curious, he opened the French doors and stepped out into the hazy morning.

"What's wrong? Couldn't you sleep?" he asked.

Patricia stared back at him, her focus steady. After a drag on her cigarette, she answered. "No, I couldn't sleep. Where are you off to?"

"Work," Nick said slowly. "Just like every morning. Friday will be my last day."

Patricia felt herself tense, but didn't say anything about his continuing to work at the diner. It galled her to no end that he was still working in that drab place, especially since she had demanded that he quit. She took a deep breath and willed herself not to say anything. *You've got to get him to agree to this. Calm down. If you do this right, the two of them will be history anyway. The fact that he worked the summer at the diner will be insignificant.*

She brought her cigarette to her lips again and nodded toward the chair across from her. "Sit down, please. I need to talk to you about something."

This time, Nick was the one who tensed. He had had many an argument with his mother, all of them beginning with that same statement. Nevertheless, he did as he was instructed, pulling out the chair from the wrought-iron patio set and dropping into it.

Forcing his voice to sound cheerful, he asked, "What is it?"

"I spoke with Natalie Mason last night." She watched Nick, trying desperately to gauge his reaction.

He shrugged without interest. "That's good. How is she?"

"Fine, fine. Her dad and her mom have been divorced for almost a year now. You know she's living with her dad, don't you? Anyway," she continued without waiting for Nick to answer, "she starts college this fall. I told her that I thought it would be nice for us to have them up, give them a chance to get out of the city. She said her father wants to go over a few stocks with me anyway." She took a break in the conversation, hoping that she wasn't talking too fast, that he wouldn't suspect anything. Her heart was racing. She was always one to keep her cool, to never give away what she was thinking or feeling, but this particular situation had her especially tense. She just had to make this work.

Nick nodded as he ran his hand through his hair. "That sounds great." He started to rise from the chair.

"I assumed that you would be excited to see her–it's been since last Christmas that they were here last, so I invited them for this coming weekend. It will be wonderful..."

"Well I'm sorry, but I won't be here," Nick interrupted. "I've got plans."

Patricia's body tensed as she forced herself to remain calm and collected. "Nonsense. What's more important than spending the weekend with Natalie? Why, the two of you practically grew up together. And besides," she said, carefully enunciating each word, "you *know* how she feels about you. It wouldn't be the same without you here. I will have *no* problem at all entertaining her father," Patricia said with a flirty bat of her eyelashes. "But there is no way I can provide her with enough to do. Only you can do that."

"What about Samantha?"

Patricia shook her head vigorously and reached for her coffee mug. "The two of them have never gotten along and you know that. It's you she asked about, and I want you to be here."

Thoughts of Maggie and his planned trip to Atlanta ran through his mind. He had so many things he wanted to show her. He wanted to make wonderful memories for her, knowing that it would be Thanksgiving break, probably, before he saw her again. Unless, of course, he got an extended weekend and could...

"Nick? What are you thinking about?" His mother interrupted his thoughts. "The upcoming weekend with Natalie, I hope," she said with a wry smile. "I don't have to remind you how beautiful she is, either, do I?"

Nick ignored her comment. Sure, Natalie was beautiful. But she was one of the girls his mother had always pushed on him. She was fake and demanding, just like his mother. Maggie was the only real beauty there was, as far as he was concerned. Once again, he declined his mother's offer. "I'm sorry, Mother, but I can't. I told you, I already have plans. There's just no way I can break them." He sighed deeply. "Tell Natalie and her father hello for me, though."

"That's not acceptable, Nicholas." Patricia's voice caught him as he tried to move away from the table. "You know that I have sacrificed a lot for you over the years. And these are good people, good *friends*, of ours. All Natalie talked about was seeing you. And we won't disappoint her. Now, whatever little plans you have, you can just cancel." She fought to control her breathing. She wanted to be adamant that he be there, but she couldn't push him too far. She had to think, to perhaps strike a bargain with him.

"I can't. I can't do that to Maggie, and I won't do it to her."

"So," Patricia hissed. "The plans you refuse to break are with *her*. Just as I thought." Her mind raced as she tried to quickly think of what else she could do. She rubbed her temples with her forefingers, trying to fight off a headache that was swiftly coming on. It would be perfect if Nick broke this important date with Maggie. Then, maybe, Maggie would begin to doubt his sincerity. Maybe she would begin to wonder if they were compatible after all.

"I have told you before how I feel about that girl," Patricia continued. "But you don't seem to think you have to listen to your own mother."

Nick tried to remain calm, but when the subject of Maggie arose, he felt himself getting worked-up. "I've told you before, the subject isn't open for discussion. It's our last weekend together since I'll be heading back to college next Wednesday. She's the one I want to spend my time with, not Natalie."

"I've told you before and I'll tell you again," Patricia retorted. "I can make your life a living hell. A nightmare. And I don't just mean financially. I mean in every *possible* way." She drew a deep breath and closed her eyes. *Stop it, Patricia. This is not the route you want to take.* She opened her eyes and looked squarely at Nick. "How about this? If you will do this one thing for me, just give me this one weekend, then I promise I will never have another bad thing to say about…Maggie, is it? I will embrace your relationship with her, in fact. It's just that this weekend means so much to me. We haven't done anything with the Masons in a while, and I really don't want Natalie to be disappointed. And believe me, she *will* be disappointed if you aren't here to spend time with her." She stopped, realizing that she was being long-winded and not giving Nick a chance to respond.

He sighed heavily. The thought of his relationship with Maggie being accepted was tempting. Even if it meant that he had to forego this one weekend with her to achieve that. But he couldn't possibly cancel his weekend with her though. She was too excited; too eager to go away with him. Knowing her, she probably already had her bags packed and ready. She would be heartbroken if he canceled. Then again, if he didn't do this one thing for his mother, he *knew* that she would make his life a living hell; he didn't doubt that she meant what she said. Maybe he could do this in order to better their future together…

He silently contemplated his choices. He stroked his chin with one hand and rested his other hand on the back of the chair in front of him. His eyes sought the gray sky as if probing it for the answer to his dilemma.

"Furthermore," Patricia added, distracting Nick momentarily from his decision, "It would only be Saturday and Saturday night. They're leaving first thing Sunday morning. How bad would one day be? Anyway, if Maggie really cares about you, she won't mind you doing something special with your family, now will she?" She added this part in a high-pitched tone as if to question Maggie's intentions once again.

"Why is this so important to you anyway, Mother? Why should you care whether or not I'm here to entertain Natalie? She's a big girl. Surely she can find something constructive to get in to." He checked his watch, making sure that he still had plenty of time before he had to leave.

Patricia thought carefully before she spoke. *It's important to me because I am going to make sure my plan gets carried out, ensuring that your relationship with this girl ends. After what will happen Saturday night, Sunday won't even matter.* But she said none of this. Instead, she lit another cigarette and took a long draw, inhaling the nicotine that her body craved deep within her lungs. After exhaling, her eyes met Nick's.

"It is important to me because I am trying to finish a business deal with *her* father that *your* father started with him not long before he died. We stand to make a lot of money…and I stress *a lot.*" She watched Nick, trying to read his expressionless face. "You know how much of a daddy's girl Natalie always has been. If it were any other way, I'm sure she would have chosen to remain with her mother after the divorce."

Nick looked at his mother and shrugged his shoulders, still unsure of where she was going with all of this. When he didn't verbally answer her, she continued.

"Think about it. If his precious daughter isn't happy and doesn't get what she wants, then he might not help me with this business deal. He's always been one to make sure his daughter has whatever she wants. Just spend the one day and evening here to make them *both* happy. Explain to your little girlfriend that it's just a family matter that you need to attend to. I promise you, they will be leaving on Sunday and you will be free to do whatever you want. If you do this for me, I will bite my tongue about your relationship with her. That's a promise." She reached for her coffee mug and took another gulp. She watched Nick for a reaction over the top of the mug. Setting it back down, she continued, "What do you say?"

Once again, Nick was at a loss for words. He considered all of the information that he had just been given. Was she telling the truth? Was the real reason she wanted him to spend time with Natalie just as she said, or was it another tactic to push him further away from Maggie? Sighing, he paced on the patio without responding. His mind reeled with the offer she had made him. What should he do? What was the *right* thing to do?

As if trying to remind him she was still there, Patricia cleared her throat loudly. "Nicholas? I'm waiting."

Nick realized that this wasn't something that he could decide on right away. He glanced at his watch briefly before he fixed his gaze on his mother. "I don't know right now. You've given me a lot to think about. I'll have to let you know sometime later in the week."

With that, Nick turned quickly and headed back inside to finish getting ready for work. Patricia remained at the patio table, a smile already spreading across her face.

The rest of the week went by in a blur. The diner was exceptionally busy, many customers stopping by to pick up large orders for one last summer barbeque. Maggie and Nick didn't have much free time to talk while they were there. They spent most evenings together, but Maggie noticed that Nick just wasn't himself. She called him on it one evening when he dropped her off after the diner closed.

They sat in Maggie's driveway in the silent truck. Nick leaned back and looked up at the black sky dotted with glittering stars. He sighed heavily. Their windows were down, and sounds of chirping crickets and cicadas filled the cab. Off in the distance, an owl hooted.

Maggie squeezed his hand. "Are you okay?"

Nick took his eyes off of the sky and focused on her, nodding. "Yeah. Why do you ask?"

Maggie shrugged. "I don't know. You just seem…reserved, that's all. What's on your mind?" Assuming that he was consumed with thoughts of having to leave, Maggie slid over closer to Nick and squeezed his hand again.

What Maggie didn't know was the decision that Nick was grappling with. He hadn't given his mother an answer yet; in fact, he hadn't spoken to her in the two days since she had propositioned him. However, his mind was constantly whirling, thinking about what he should do. Maggie had brought up their scheduled weekend trip several times, and Nick had just listened to her gush without responding.

Now, Nick thought carefully about what he should say to Maggie. Should he go ahead and tell her that he had something come up for Saturday and that the trip she was so looking forward to would have to be canceled? Or should he instead tell his mother to forget it, that he was spending the weekend with Maggie anyway, knowing what kind of problems his mother would cause after that? Sighing deeply, Nick squeezed Maggie's hand back. "I'm okay. You know I have to be going back to college soon, that's just really been on my mind."

"I figured that's what's got you so upset. Well, you're here now," Maggie said with a giggle as she leaned over to kiss Nick on the lips. "Let's not think of it right now."

Unintentionally, he pulled away from her. He felt guilty about not telling her of the dilemma he was in. Maybe it would have made it easier if he had told her the truth about his mother from the start, of how his mother *really* felt about his relationship with her. Now, because he hadn't been completely honest, it made it more difficult to say anything at all.

Hurt by his reaction to her kiss, Maggie slid her hand away and reached for the door handle on the passenger side. "I guess I'll be going now."

Nick simply nodded in response. Then, for the first time since they met, Maggie walked to the front door alone. Nick waited until she was safely inside before he drove away, his head swimming with a thousand thoughts and one massive decision that he must make.

Once inside, Maggie shut the door carefully and locked it. She heard her grandmother puttering around in the kitchen, and Maggie yelled out briefly to let her know that she was home. Heading upstairs, Maggie went into the bathroom and ran a tub full of warm water and bath salts. Climbing in to the steamy liquid, she settled back against the cool porcelain and closed her eyes.

What was going on with Nick? There was definitely something different about him these past few days. Ordinarily at work, he would wink at her in passing when they were really busy, or make a silly face at her to make her laugh when no one else could see. But lately he did nothing of the sort. Instead, he concentrated fully on each task, his mouth set firmly in determination. He didn't crack jokes with any of the customers, and he didn't come into the kitchen before closing and rub Maggie's shoulders while she was washing dishes like he normally did. Instead, he furiously scrubbed tables until his hands were raw and restocked items until he was breathless. Maggie had teasingly mentioned to him earlier that he could slow down, but he hadn't responded.

Maggie wondered if his going back to college was the only thing on his mind. Sighing, Maggie opened her eyes and looked around the tiny bathroom. As much as she tried not to think about it, memories of her conversation with Nick's mother crept back into her mind. She remembered the part of the conversation that she had tried so desperately to push away. *I'm not surprised to see you here so late. Nick does this sort of thing often, entertaining beautiful women at all hours.* Maggie closed her eyes tightly and ground the heels of her hands into them. Could that be the reason Nick was so distant? Did he have other girlfriends on the side, perhaps a girlfriend back at college, and he was trying to shrug Maggie off before he headed back?

Stop it! She willed herself to quit being so negative. Maybe he's right–he just has going back to school on his mind. Regardless of the reason, the change was noticeable and extremely puzzling.

Trying to forget about it for the moment, Maggie allowed her arms to float up to the surface of the warm water. She felt so relaxed that she didn't want to move. Eventually the water turned cooler, and she stepped out to towel off. The window in the bathroom was open slightly and a breeze blew in, chilling her.

After getting her pajamas on and crawling between clean, cool sheets, Maggie decided that she was just being paranoid. There was no way she had imagined the great times she had spent with Nick this summer. She made up her mind to quit questioning Nick, and to give him some space. When he was ready, he would talk to her…just like he had at numerous other times.

    That decided, Maggie rolled over and closed her eyes. Everything was just fine, of that she was certain.

CHAPTER 14

Nick tossed and turned all night. He realized that he was acting strangely toward Maggie, and he hated himself for it. He just had so much on his mind, weighing his options and trying to make the best decision.

The more he had thought about it over the past two days, the more he was leaning toward doing as his mother wished. At least she would quit harassing him about Maggie, and he could more than make up for canceling out on a date with Maggie. That made the most sense, didn't it?

At four o'clock, exhausted yet unable to sleep, Nick climbed out of bed and into a long, warm shower. The water felt good and invigorating, yet when he got out and toweled off, the same troubles came right back to him. Nothing, he realized, was going to make them go away.

Heading downstairs, he put on a pot of strong coffee and went outside to see if the day's paper had arrived. As he came back inside, he saw his mother coming down the winding staircase in the foyer.

"Nicholas? What is it? I heard the door."

"Nothing," Nick responded. "I couldn't sleep."

Continuing down the stairs, Patricia followed him into the kitchen and pulled out a chair from the breakfast table. Sitting down abruptly and crossing her legs, she asked the question that Nick knew she would.

"Have you made up your mind yet about Saturday?"

Tensing slightly as he pulled out a chair opposite his mother, Nick surprised himself by his answer. "I've done a lot of thinking about it. And I guess one day away from Maggie wouldn't hurt. But I'll do this only, and I mean *only*, if you meant what you said about leaving me and Maggie alone." He paused, his eyes fixed steadily on his mother. "I'm serious Mother. If I do this and you betray me…" His voice trailed off.

Patricia shook her head side to side earnestly. "You have my word. If you do this, then I promise I will leave you and Maggie alone." Standing, she smiled broadly at Nick and patted his shoulder as she walked past him out of the kitchen. "You won't regret this. You and Natalie will have a wonderful time."

Nick, feeling relieved that his decision was made yet still feeling apprehensive about what he had done, hung his head and exhaled slowly. Now the hard part would be breaking the news to Maggie.

Nick tried to make a conscious effort that day at work to be more upbeat and talkative. He knew that his demeanor had given Maggie reason to be concerned over the past few days. He felt nervous, though, about how and when he would break the news to her. Not having too much time to talk during the day, he didn't have much of a chance to worry about it. At one point, as Nick waited on a customer at the counter, Maggie walked past him behind the counter and whispered, "I love you." It was hardly audible, but Nick heard it all the same.

Nick smiled faintly at her as she went past, feeling terrible about what he was going to do. But it was for a good reason, he told himself. That was the *only* reason he was going ahead with this.

That evening, Nick took Maggie to eat at a Mexican restaurant after the diner closed. He planned to tell her then about the weekend, but it was once again too difficult. Maggie talked enthusiastically over chips and salsa, then continued talking between bites of food once their entrées arrived. She told stories of fishing with her grandfather when she was a child and somehow wound up talking about his funeral.

Nick hardly had an appetite, yet he forced himself to eat so that Maggie wouldn't notice that anything was wrong. He thought again how beautiful she was. She talked using her hands, which Nick had always found endearing. She constantly tucked her hair behind one ear. She had a habit of wrinkling up her cute nose when she laughed.

Nick impulsively reached out and touched Maggie's hand, and she stopped talking briefly to look deep into Nick's eyes. Instinctively, she saw something there that she couldn't quite put her finger on.

"Nick?" she asked softly. "Are you okay?" Maggie realized that he still hadn't been acting like himself lately. Sure, they had still been spending time together each evening. But now that she paused to reflect, she realized that *she* had been doing all of the talking, all of the communicating. It hit her like a punch in the stomach that Nick seemed to be slowly and deliberately withdrawing from her.

Nick sighed heavily. It hurt him to the core what he was about to say, yet what choice did he have? No, after weighing all of his options for days now, he still came to the same conclusion. He was doing this for the good of both of them. It was *one day*, he told himself. One day in a lifetime didn't seem like much.

After a long time with no response, Maggie reached out and touched the back of Nick's hand gently. "Nick?"

Nick gradually raised his eyes to meet Maggie's, hers resembling two emeralds lighting up the delicate features of her face. "There's something I need to tell you."

Maggie inhaled sharply. *Okay, here goes*, Maggie told herself. *I don't think I can handle a long distance relationship. And since it's almost time for me to go back to college...* She braced herself for the words that never came.

"I...I'm afraid I have to break our date for this weekend." There. He had said it. The dreaded words were out.

Maggie, expecting to hear something else, almost laughed in relief. "Excuse me?"

Nick began talking, almost too quickly, trying to get out the words that he had rehearsed over and over in his head. "It's this thing my mother has. Some very close friends of ours, people that we haven't seen in quite a while, are coming in town this weekend. She pretty much threatened my life if I wasn't there." He tried to laugh, but it came out sounding forced. "Anyway, it's mostly just for Saturday, so we can still have Sunday together. And I've already asked about having you over." Nick hung his head, too embarrassed to look

Maggie in the eye. "Well...my mother doesn't want any other company. She can be weird about that sometimes."

Maggie sat silently as Nick got it all off his chest. She absentmindedly twisted her napkin in her lap without being cognizant of it. As he finished speaking and exhaled, Maggie reached over and touched him once again. "Is that why you've been acting so strange lately? You were afraid to tell me?"

Nick nodded. "I feel just awful about this, Maggie. I don't want to do this, but my mother *did* bring up the fact that she hasn't asked me to spend any time with her all summer. And you have my *word* that we can do whatever you want to do on Sunday. We can still drive to Atlanta then, if you want."

Maggie smiled sweetly at him and shook her head. "No, that's okay. I would have liked to have gone, but it's important, too, that you be with your family." She said it with more conviction than she actually felt.

Nick reached across the dimly lit table and cupped Maggie's chin in his strong hand. He knew now, without a doubt, that he loved Maggie with his entire heart and soul. She had accepted the unpleasant news with fervor, something that he himself wasn't sure that *he* could have done.

"I love you, Maggie."

"I love you too."

"I mean it," he said. "I love you more than anything. And I promise you, I *will* make this up to you."

Maggie shrugged it off. "It's no big deal, Nick. I understand. It's not like you're choosing between me and your family." *Is it?*

Nick stood then and helped Maggie to her feet. He paid the bill, then held the door for her as they walked out into the autumn evening. Although the weather wasn't quite turning cool yet, it was breezy, and after leaving the restaurant Maggie shivered slightly. Nick quickly put his arm around her and pulled her close. The moon, now milky white and high in the sky, shone down upon them as they walked through the practically empty parking lot to Nick's truck.

They rode in silence for the majority of the short trip. As Nick turned onto Azalea Lane, Maggie looked up at Nick's profile, and knew that he must care an awful lot about her if he had been that worried about upsetting her.

"Nick?"

"Hmmm?"

They pulled into the driveway and Maggie turned toward him slowly. "I don't ever want to lose you." She grabbed him in a secure embrace, surprising him, and instinctively his arms encircled her in return, something that felt natural and right for the both of them. Maggie squeezed tightly. She shuddered at the thought of what she had assumed Nick might have told her tonight. She realized now that the thought of his leaving, of being away from him, scared her to death.

After several moments, Nick was the first to pull away. Peering down into Maggie's deep green eyes, he finally replied. "Don't ever, *ever*, worry about that. Please. I want to be with you forever, Maggie. Don't ever doubt that."

Nick purposely didn't mention the word marriage. He had been thinking a lot about it lately, and he had decided that he would ask her to be his wife when he came come for Christmas. In fact, he had been looking around at rings during the few times he had been away from Maggie.

He knew that they were young, and that they hadn't known each other for an incredible amount of time. And he was prepared to hear all of the negative comments from friends and family alike, once he proposed and she hopefully accepted, so he had already begun mentally compiling his argument. He knew in his heart that they belonged together. They shared the same interests; they felt comfortable in each other's presence. He never felt obligated to talk just to fill the silence when he was around Maggie...sometimes a comfortable silence descended upon them and no words needed to be spoken in order to convey what they were feeling.

Now, he didn't want to say anything about marriage and ruin the surprise he had planned for later. Because of this, he had been choosing his words to her very carefully.

SIMPLE THINGS

He kissed her tenderly on the top of her head as he pulled her close. "I mean it. Nothing can break us apart."
Maggie locked eyes with Nick. "Good. Then I feel better already."

CHAPTER 15

Although her grandmother was awake when Maggie got home, Maggie remained silent about the conversation she had had with Nick that evening. She *was* disappointed, of that it was certain, but she would have the chance Saturday to get some much needed things done, run some errands, and spend some general time alone. She knew, without a doubt, that if she told her grandmother about not being able to spend the weekend with Nick, she would want to cancel her trip to Ruth's, choosing instead to spend the weekend cheering Maggie up. Maggie would appreciate her grandma's sincere efforts, yet she didn't want her grandmother to cancel plans on her account. The time alone would be welcomed as well. Besides, there was always Sunday with Nick.

Feeling a little sad and disappointed; yet relieved that Nick's distant behavior over the past few days was so easily explained, Maggie peeled off her clothes in the bathroom and turned the shower knobs until a steady stream of hot water sprayed from the nozzle. She piled her blond hair loosely on top of her head and then stepped in, allowing the pounding of the water to massage her aching muscles. It was there, amidst the steam and the flowing water, that the tears she had held back for so long began to flow as well.

The next day at the diner was the slowest of the season. Maggie was relieved for the break, and she could tell that Nick was as well. He seemed a little more relaxed to Maggie; she was sure that it was because he had finally shared with her the news that had disturbed him over the past several days. She knew that it always made you feel better when you got something off of your chest.

Maggie felt more like herself this morning. Although her eyes had still been a little red-rimmed when she awoke, it was nothing that some Visine and a little make-up couldn't fix. She understood Nick's predicament, truly she did...she just really had been looking forward to the trip, and looking forward to spending a romantic weekend away with Nick. Although she had stood strong, and had told Nick that he was doing the right thing, she wasn't sure if she really felt that way at all.

She quickly shook that feeling off, however, when she saw Nick again that morning, looking handsome in his faded jeans and t-shirt. He had a dark tan that had accumulated over the summer, which made his sky blue eyes appear even lighter, if that were possible. He had hugged her tightly and told her he loved her before asking if she was *sure* that she was okay about his change of plans. Maggie, of course, had assured him that she was fine with it.

As if the weather realized that it was Nick's last day as well, the sky grew dark and the rain began to come down in torrents. Thunder boomed loudly and the lights flickered a time or two. Maggie wished secretly that she and Nick were cuddled up together at the cabin, under the big quilt in front of a crackling fire instead of being here at the diner.

A half hour before the diner was set to close at the noon hour, Maggie disappeared to the back. She came out carrying a red velvet cake, Nick's favorite, with *We'll miss you, Nick!* written across it in red glazed icing. Nick crossed his arms and shook his head, surprised and touched at the same time. Several of the regular customers had stopped by as well, all with words of praise for Nick.

Several people even brought parting gifts: an engraved pen, a pre-paid calling card 'so you can call this little gal whenever you want', a sweatshirt embroidered with *Cedar Creek*. Lily handed over her gift last...inside, Nick found a snapshot of him and Maggie, arms around each other and their cheeks touching, that Lily had enlarged to an eight-by-ten and had matted and framed. As everyone else dug into cake and ice cream, Nick held the picture close to his chest and mouthed a silent 'thank you' to Lily, who was standing several feet away. Lily simply nodded her response, a warm smile on her face.

Maggie made sure that everyone had a piece of cake before she got one for herself and moved over to sit beside Nick in the back booth. Ruth Anne had been sitting there and quickly jumped up.

"Here honey, you can have my seat. I'm all finished anyway."

Maggie took the spot and took a bite of the moist cake. She leaned over closer to Nick's ear and whispered, "I didn't forget your present...I just can't give it to you in front of anyone." She giggled.

With a knowing smile, Nick responded. "Well, maybe we should get rid of everyone."

As if hearing his words, the last of the group began to move out, all stopping over to give Nick one last hug, handshake, or pat on the back. The rain was still steady, and a few paused at the doorway to open their umbrellas.

As Lily began picking up the mess that had been strewn about, Nick asked Maggie if she wanted to do anything together that afternoon.

"After all," he added, "it's still early. And you *do* have to give me that present, you know," he elbowed her lightly in the ribs, teasing her.

Maggie smiled back and put her elbow on the table, cupping her chin in the palm of her hand. "I would like to, but I promised my grandmother that I would help her gather her things and take her and her friend to the bus station. By the time I get all of that done, I'm afraid it will be pretty late," she said with obvious regret.

"Oh. Why are they taking the bus?"

Maggie shrugged. "Grandma never has been one that liked to fly. And Savannah is way too far for her to drive by herself, which is what she'd have to do since Ellen doesn't drive at all."

Nick nodded in understanding as he took a drink of tea.

"Maybe Sunday, if we don't do anything else, you can go with me to look at cars," Maggie said, changing the subject. "I don't think the dealers are open then, but at least I can try to decide on what I want."

Nick nodded again and rubbed the palms of his hands on his jeans. "So you want a car of your own, huh?"

"Yeah. That's what I've been saving my money for this past year. I know Grandma doesn't mind me driving her truck, but..." Her voice trailed off. "I just don't want to take advantage, you know?"

Once again, Nick felt guilty. His first car, a Firebird, had been a gift for his sixteenth birthday. As a graduation present from high school, he had been allowed to trade it in on a truck of his choice, the full-sized Ford that he now drove. He wondered if these were the kinds of things his mother was talking about when she had said that he and Maggie weren't compatible. Nick quickly shrugged that thought off, unsure of where it had come from.

About that time, Lily came from the back kitchen and started flipping lights off. "Are you two ready to go, or do you want to sit here in the dark?"

The two quickly jumped up and helped Lily finish closing. At the back door, Lily headed to the truck but, as usual, Nick and Maggie lingered behind.

Nick reached for Maggie's hand, drawing her closer to him. "So, will you be okay? You need me to ride along?"

Maggie shook her head. "No, we'll be fine. You enjoy your evening. I'm sure you won't know how to act, being alone for once," she said with a soft laugh.

"I guess I won't see you until Sunday, then," Nick said with disappointment. "I'll be thinking of you every second though."

Maggie nodded. "Same here. But have a good time. I mean it. And tell your mom and sister hello for me."

"I will." Nick shoved his hands into the front pockets of his jeans. He wanted to kiss her so badly, but with Lily waiting in the truck, he was almost afraid to.

As if sensing his hesitation, Maggie stood on her tip-toes and kissed Nick softly and quickly on the lips. With that, she turned in the direction of the truck and walked away, her eyes watching the ground as she took each step.

CHAPTER 16

Later that evening, after seeing her grandmother and Ellen off safely at the bus station, Maggie was unsure of what to do or where to go. She checked her watch. Seven thirty five. She could always stop by Nick's house and surprise him...

No, she decided. He had mentioned earlier that his mom had asked for some help around the house before their company came. Since his mother had specifically denied his request for Maggie to attend, she would feel out of place just showing up. That never had been her style.

She wondered silently about his company that was coming. Nick hadn't mentioned them by name, nor had he told her anything about them. Oh well, it didn't really matter, did it? She was missing out on a whole day that she could have spent with Nick, and that was the only way that she saw it.

Driving the twenty miles back to Cedar Creek gave Maggie a lot of time to think. She remembered how she had felt before meeting Nick...she hadn't wanted to get involved with anyone, especially seriously, and now...

Well, now she couldn't imagine life without him. She smiled at the thought of him, seeing images of him in her mind. She saw him dancing at the cabin to make her laugh, the painstaking way he had set up the picnic to surprise her, the look in his eyes as they made love. If she thought hard enough, she could almost feel his strong arms around her and could almost smell the faint scent of his cologne.

Taking a deep breath, Maggie realized that she definitely loved Nick Winters. *More than life itself.*

On impulse, Maggie pulled into a shopping center a few miles from home and rented a movie, a comedy, with the hopes that it would cheer her up. After paying for the movie rental, she placed the video in her bag and walked next door and picked up a sub sandwich for dinner. It was never any fun to cook for one. Besides, she really wasn't that hungry, anyway.

She slipped back into the driver's seat and pulled out of the parking lot, her mind still on thoughts of Nick. Maggie carefully guided the truck around a curve in the road, not knowing that life as she knew it was about to be changed forever.

That evening, Patricia had a hard time relaxing. The house, completely spotless, had been cleaned earlier by the housekeeper. She had gone above and beyond the normal routine. The windows had been shined, the silver polished. When Patricia was satisfied with the appearance of things, she had promptly dismissed Rosie, giving her a healthy tip.

All of the pieces were falling into place beautifully. She had been in touch with Natalie earlier; both she and her father would be arriving early in the morning. She had plans of entertaining them pool side for the first part of the day. The weather was calling for rain again, however, and if that happened, she would have to change her plans quickly.

And Nick. He had come through for her, canceling his plans with Maggie like she had requested. Now she had to wait until the elegant dinner she had planned for tomorrow evening, and hope that everything continued to move as smoothly.

There was just one more thing she had to do yet, a phone call that she needed to make. She had just sent Nick to the store to buy a few last minute food items. It was important that she know Nick's whereabouts before she made this call. She didn't want him anywhere around, just to make certain he didn't overhear anything.

Downing the last of her second glass of wine, Patricia reached for the phone. She had looked up the number she needed earlier, and now, she pulled the slip of paper from inside of the book she had tucked it into. She took a deep breath and began to punch the numbers carefully.

Maggie had barely unlocked the door and was trying to balance her bags when the phone began ringing. *It must be Ruth,* she thought, *calling to make sure Grandma got off okay.*

"Hold on, don't hang up!" she yelled to the ringing phone. Placing her bags and keys on the stand in the foyer, she ran to the kitchen to pick up the extension.

"Hello?"

"Maggie, please." The voice was a woman's, older, and though somewhat familiar, Maggie couldn't quite place it.

"Speaking."

The voice warmed. "Oh, hello, dear. I thought that was you. It's Patricia...Nick's mother."

Startled, Maggie sucked in a breath. "Hello, Mrs. Winters. Is everything okay? Is Nick..."

"Oh, sure, everything's fine," she interrupted. "I was just calling to see how you were. Nick never brings you around," she said with an abrupt laugh.

Maggie had a hard time containing her surprise. "Oh...well...I know, I've been meaning to go over, but we've been so busy..." Her voice trailed.

"I know, I know. That's how we all are these days."

There was an uncomfortable pause, and Maggie wondered the real reason for the phone call. Absentmindedly, she twirled the long phone cord around her forefinger.

"Listen, I'm having a dinner tomorrow evening, and I'd like you to come."

Maggie, once again, was speechless. Nick had specifically told her that his mother didn't want any other company, and here she was being invited by Mrs. Winters herself. She didn't know what to make of it. Well, Mrs. Winters could have changed her mind, couldn't she?

"Umm...I..." Maggie stammered.

"Please say yes." Patricia was persistent.

Finally finding her voice and composing herself, Maggie answered slowly. "Nick mentioned the dinner. But..."

"But what?"

"He also mentioned that it was just for your guests and family. I was under the impression that I wasn't invited." There. The words were out. How would Mrs. Winters respond to that?

Patricia laughed, deep and throaty. "Well, I don't know where he got *that* idea," she said bluntly.

Maggie felt her blood turn cold and her knees go weak. *Had Nick simply misunderstood his mother? Or could it be possible that Nick didn't want her there?*

"Oh…" It was about all Maggie could manage to say.

"Well?"

"Oh, I don't know, Mrs. Winters," she started. "I had made other plans," she lied. Well, it wasn't a lie *exactly*…she had planned to run errands. But it was nothing that couldn't be easily changed.

"Well if you can't come for dinner, at least come by for dessert. Say…around seven thirty or eight tomorrow evening?"

Maggie considered what she should do. It *would* be nice to spend some time with Nick, and to get to know his family better as well. She was still contemplating what she should do when she was interrupted again.

"Are you there?"

"Oh, yes, Mrs. Winters. I'm here. I…" Maggie stammered momentarily. "I would love to," she said finally. "But I can only be there for dessert." That way, Maggie figured, she wouldn't wear out her welcome, and they would be able to visit with their company before she ever arrived.

"Wonderful," Patricia shouted. "I'll see you tomorrow evening, then, hmm?"

"That sounds great. Good-bye, Mrs. Winters."

"Oh, wait. Maggie?"

"Yes?"

"If you talk to Nick beforehand, don't mention that I called. We'll keep your arrival a secret, shall we? It will be great fun to surprise him."

Maggie smiled into the phone, feeling that she and Nick's mother were bonding. "Okay," she answered softly. "I'll keep it a secret." With that, the line went dead in her ear.

CHAPTER 17

Nick felt like he was a million miles away the next morning. He awoke early and showered, wondering if Maggie was awake yet as well. He started to call her but on second thought changed his mind. If she had decided to sleep late, he didn't want to be the one to wake her. She had mentioned the previous afternoon how tired she was.

As he toweled off after his shower, he heard voices and commotion downstairs. Before he could get dressed, he heard his mother shout, "Nick! Natalie's here!"

Nick rolled his eyes as he pulled a shirt on over his head. He had always resented being around Natalie, mainly because his mother pushed her on him. And also because Natalie was so demanding and so...well, *annoying*.

Realizing that he couldn't put it off any longer, Nick towel dried his hair, combed it, brushed his teeth, and slowly descended down the stairs.

Natalie practically attacked Nick before he reached the foyer downstairs. She threw her arms around him and buried her face in the nape of his neck. Nick patted her back once for politeness and then tried to pry her off.

Stepping back, Natalie grabbed both of his hands and squeezed tightly. "Just look at *you*!" she gushed. "You look so handsome! I had no idea you would have changed so much in less than a year." She squeezed his hands again before stepping up to plant a kiss on Nick's cheek. "You were always good looking, of course, but now you just look unbelievable."

Nick, embarrassed by the show of attention, shrugged. He smiled nervously, feeling uncomfortable with the situation he was in. Then: "How've you been?"

"Oh, just *wonderful*," she drawled in a slow southern accent.

"Can't you tell? Look at me." She stood back and held her arms out, turning a slow circle three hundred and sixty degrees.

Nick watched her as she did this. She *was* beautiful, no doubt about it. Her silky auburn hair hung down to her waist. Her complexion was flawless, as was her make-up and fingernails. Her attire, all the way to her shoes and handbag, had designer labels.

About all of this, Nick didn't care. He could only think about Maggie and wonder what she was doing. Was she still in bed, curled up and dreaming? Was she having pancakes, her favorite breakfast in the world? Was she sitting on the front porch, sipping coffee and reading the morning paper? Was she thinking about him?

"Well answer me, silly," Natalie interrupted, hands on hips.

Natalie's voice brought him out of his reverie. He rubbed his eyes and shook his head, trying to clear his mind. "You've definitely grown up," Nick said for lack of anything else.

Natalie took this as something positive. "Yes I have," she breathed. "And in more ways than *one.*"

Nick didn't miss the seductiveness in her voice. He shuddered at the thought of spending the day with Natalie. It was definitely going to be a long one.

Nick tried later in the day to corner his mother, to tell her that the deal was off, but every time he started to, he lost his nerve. He just kept reminding himself of the reason he was doing this. *Maggie.* He only had to think of her, to picture her beautiful face in his mind, to realize that he had to go through with this. After all, he had made it this far, and he was not going to give up now.

Entertaining Natalie proved to be quite a challenge. She spent the morning catching Nick up on the latest gossip on all of her friends, none of whom Nick knew, and he could have cared less. Nonetheless, he tried to sound interested, asking assorted questions or adding comments. He tried to keep his distance from her, to treat her like the little sister he had always seen her as, but she was persistent.

She curled up next to Nick on the sofa when he put a movie in to watch. He inched away from her little by little, but she would slide over as well, until he was sandwiched between her and the arm of the couch. He quickly jumped up and made the excuse that he needed to get them something to drink.

When he came back into the family room, he sat Natalie's soda can on the end table and this time flopped down on an oversized chair, kicking his feet up on the matching ottoman. Natalie immediately followed suit, picking herself up off of the sofa and sitting on the ottoman in front of him.

"Nick? Can I be honest with you?" Natalie pouted her full lips and tossed her auburn mane over her shoulder. With a perfect fingernail she began to trace tiny circles on his leg.

Shaking her off, Nick jumped up again. Standing to face her, he glared down at her. "What, Natalie?!" He didn't try to hide the irritation in his voice.

"Well…" she began. "You know how I always used to tell you that I was going to marry you when I grew up?" She stood up and started walking at a slow pace toward him. Nick continued to take gradual steps backward.

"Yeah, so? You were *ten*." Nick forced a laugh, even though the situation he was in was *not* humorous.

Natalie shook her head and smiled alluringly as she faced Nick. "I know…but deep down, I was serious." She cleared her throat, tossed her hair over her shoulder once again for effect. "I know we've grown apart these past few years, Nick. But my feelings have never changed. I think about you all the time. I dream about you. I just want you to give me, to give *us*, a chance. I think the two of us would be great together, don't you?"

Nick stared at her, unable to believe the words that were coming out of her mouth. Did his mother put her up to this? She was coming on awfully strong.

He shook his head and put his hand out to push her back. She was invading his space, and he didn't like her being that close to him. All he could think about was Maggie, and he felt guilty for just being here with Natalie, all though nothing had, or *would,* happen between them.

"Wait a minute," Nick said as he ran his fingers through his hair.

"Where is all of this coming from?"

"I've just missed you, that's all," Natalie said in a soft, innocent voice. "None of the other guys I've gone out with even come close to comparing to you." Natalie pouted her lips and reached up to touch Nick's face. He instantly recoiled as if he had been burned.

"Stop it, Natalie. I mean it." He pushed her hand away.

"Oh, come on, Nick," she purred. "Surely you've missed me too."

"I have a girlfriend, Natalie." Nick spoke the words slowly, evenly, hoping that it would be all he needed to say. He knew better, though. "Surely my mother told you about her when you two spoke on the phone?"

Natalie shrugged. "No, I don't think so. But it doesn't matter." She lunged for Nick and hugged him tightly around his waist. "I've got you for today. And where is *she*, huh?"

To this, Nick did not respond.

The rest of the day passed just as painfully for Nick. His mother spent time entertaining Natalie's father, going over her "investments." Nick hated to watch his mother in action, flirting so overtly with Jim. She reminded him of the way Natalie was acting. Or did Natalie just remind him of his mother? Regardless, it was embarrassing, and almost unbearable to observe.

Although it was overcast and threatening rain, Patricia went ahead with her noontime plans to grill on the patio. Rosie came over to do the cooking, as she usually did for special occasions.

Nick, in no mood to swim and having no appetite either, rested in a lounge chair, fully clothed, and closed his eyes. He wondered again what Maggie was up to. He hoped that everything he was going through today was well worth it in the long run. He managed a small smile as he imagined him telling her about this one day, probably after they were married. Or maybe he wouldn't tell her, who knows? Even after the fact, he wouldn't want to cause her pain. And he was sure that it would desperately hurt her feelings if she knew how his mother had felt all along about her.

Lost in thought, he didn't hear Natalie approach. She flung cold water on him and he jumped, sitting up quickly.

"What the..." He lowered his shades and peered at her. She was the only one dressed for swimming, in a turquoise bikini that left very little to the imagination. Embarrassed, Nick quickly put his shades back on and looked away.

"What's the matter, Nick?" Natalie called, taunting him. "Ashamed because you like what you see?"

Nick ignored her.

Natalie leaned her face down close to Nick's. She was close enough that he could smell the cinnamon gum on her breath. "Don't worry, sweetheart...I'll never tell what's her name." With that, Natalie walked to the diving board of the deep end of the pool and executed a perfect leap.

CHAPTER 18

Maggie had an enjoyable day by herself. She slept soundly until eight, made pancakes for breakfast, drank coffee on the front porch while she read the morning paper, and thought about Nick off and on all day.

She wondered how his day was going with his company and if he was thinking of her as well.

She occupied her time by straightening up the house although it was really pretty neat already. She watered the flowers outside and on the porch, then decided that her grandmother's truck was in need of being washed, so she did that too.

All the while, she thought about the phone call from Mrs. Winters last night. She found it a bit odd that she had been dating Nick all summer, yet Mrs. Winters hadn't tried to contact her before now. She shrugged to herself. It didn't matter that it had taken her this long to call...Maggie was just glad that she had. It really meant a lot to her that she had been invited.

And that was another thing that was bugging her. Why had Nick said that his mother didn't want any other visitors, yet Mrs. Winters had denied saying that?

No matter how long she thought about it, she couldn't find a logical explanation. The only thing she could imagine was that Nick had misunderstood her. Or maybe Mrs. Winters *had* told Nick that she didn't want Maggie there, only to throw him off guard because she had every intention of calling Maggie to invite her as a surprise to Nick. And maybe she was just embarrassed when Maggie confronted her about it, because Mrs. Winters hadn't thought that Nick would tell Maggie what she had said.

Yes, that must be it!

Feeling better about it, Maggie settled down on the couch to watch the movie that she had rented the night before but had been too distracted to watch. She wanted to do anything possible to pass the time until it was time to leave for Nick's. She couldn't wait to see his face when she arrived.

The afternoon soon passed into evening, and Nick had had about all he could take. He did manage, at one point, to pull his mother aside and tell her that Natalie was driving him crazy.

"Oh, Nick," Patricia had said with a wave of her hand, "Don't be so serious. Lighten up, have fun. That's probably what your *girlfriend* is doing right now, don't you think?"

"I just can't take much more of her, that's all," Nick said. "I just can't."

But Patricia hadn't heard him. She was already rushing to the bar to pour another drink for Jim and herself.

He did manage to get a little bit of time alone when Natalie went to shower sometime in the afternoon before dinner. Exhausted, Nick locked the door to his room and fell into a fast slumber across the bed.

He wasn't sure how long he had been sleeping when he heard his mother calling. The room had grown darker, shadows on the ceiling and walls had moved, and Nick heard the rain pouring down from outside his window. He sat up, rubbed his eyes, and checked the clock on the bed stand. Five fifty eight, which meant he'd been sleeping for about an hour. He opened the door to his room and yelled down the stairs.

"I'll be down. Just give me a few minutes, okay?"

"Well hurry up!" his mother shouted back. "Dinner will be served in about twenty minutes."

Nick turned the water on in the shower and waited for it to warm up. While he did so, he impulsively picked up the phone and dialed Maggie's number. He wanted to hear her voice, if even for a second.

He hung up on the fifth ring.

Casting thoughts of Maggie aside temporarily, he quickly showered and dressed in khaki dress pants and a white short-sleeved button down shirt. His mother had specifically told him earlier to wear "something decent" to dinner.

He descended the stairs slowly, anxious to get this last part of the evening over with, yet dreading it all the same.

Maggie had fallen asleep on the couch, exhausted and unable to concentrate her thoughts on the movie she had tried to watch. She awoke to rain pouring outside the windows, dark shadows cast around the room in eerie patterns. She sat up quickly, her heart racing, afraid that she had overslept. She reached over and clicked on the small lamp on the end table, waited for her eyes to adjust to the light, and glanced at the mantle clock to check the time. Six twenty six.

Letting out a sigh of relief that it wasn't quite as late as she had feared, Maggie stood and stretched her arms up above her head. She walked the short distance to the television set and clicked off the snowy screen. She couldn't help but smile to herself at the thought of seeing Nick. She was excited about seeing him, of surprising him.

This was the longest she had gone without seeing him *or* talking to him since they had met. It bothered her, a little, that he hadn't called her at all today. She had picked up the phone a time or two and had almost dialed his number, but for some reason she hung up before she completed the call. She figured that he was busy, or he would have called her first. Surely he would have.

Now Maggie excitedly hurried upstairs to prepare for her evening. She hadn't asked Mrs. Winters what she should wear. Was it casual? Semi-formal? Sighing, she pushed through clothes in her tiny closet in search of the perfect outfit. Sadly, there was not much to choose from.

Finally, she decided to wear the same outfit that she had worn to Samantha's graduation. It was a nice dress, yet not too extreme one way or the other. Pleased with her choice, yet hoping that it wouldn't be tacky to wear the same dress again, Maggie placed the dress carefully across her bed and headed into the bathroom to get ready.

CHAPTER 19

The longer the dinner went, the more disgusted Nick got with the situation he found himself in. He wasn't sure how many courses to the meal there were, he lost count after the salads and shrimp cocktail. The lights were dimmed and candles were lit on the long mahogany table. His mother laughed painfully loud over and over, continuing to lean closer to Jim with each word she spoke.

Natalie, on the other hand, was all over him. She rubbed his leg under the table, squeezed him on the knee, tried to lean over and whisper in his ear. Nick continually fought her off, pushing her hand away and trying desperately to tune her out. *Just a few more hours,* he told himself. *This will all be over. And I will be free to live my life with Maggie.*

Finally, Nick had had enough. He jumped up, headed for the bar, and poured himself a shot of whiskey, downing it quickly. He cringed slightly as the liquid burned his throat. He wasn't one to drink hard liquor on a regular basis. In fact, he couldn't remember the last time he had even had a mixed drink. Now, he felt like he couldn't help himself. He would do anything to help this evening pass more quickly or more pleasantly. He knew that drinking wasn't the answer, but at this point he was running out of options.

Pouring more in a large tumbler with ice, he headed back to the table, where Natalie sat smiling up at him and batting her long eyelashes. His mother hadn't even noticed that he'd gotten up.

Nick flopped back into his seat and tossed down a bit more of the whiskey. This time it didn't quite burn so badly. After a few more sips, Nick felt his body loosen and relax slightly. He closed his eyes and tried to concentrate on Maggie. He could see her beautiful, angelic face in front of him. *I'm going to see you soon,* he thought. *This is almost over.*

As if trying to purposely destroy his pleasant thoughts, Natalie leaned in closer to him, brushing her full breasts against his arm. "What do you say we get out of here? Let's go for a walk."

Nick tossed down the last of his whiskey and narrowed his eyes at her. "It's pouring down rain. Or haven't you noticed?"

Natalie squeezed his arm lightly and traced a line down to his wrist with her fingernail. "That's okay...it's more romantic in the rain." She smiled seductively.

"I don't think so, Natalie," Nick said as he started to rise, holding on to his empty tumbler.

"Here, let me get that for you," Natalie said as she took the glass from him. "Whiskey, is it?" She sashayed toward the bar and tossed her head back over her shoulder to wink at Nick.

Nick stood, anxious to disappear. Patricia turned to him, as if suddenly aware of his presence. "And just where do you think you are going?"

"Outside. I need some fresh air." He headed out of the dining room.

"But what about Natalie..." Patricia called out.

"I'm right here," Natalie said as she hurried to catch up with Nick. "We're both going."

"Well you two have fun. Don't do anything I wouldn't do," she said with a wink to Natalie.

Natalie hurried through the dimly lit house to catch up with Nick. "Nick, wait!" she called out. "I have your whiskey. Don't you want it?"

Outside on the patio, Nick stopped and turned toward Natalie. He felt obligated to wait on her. "Well hurry up. This rain's not letting up." He felt warm and tingly all over, the effects of the whiskey already apparent.

Excited, Natalie handed him the full tumbler of whiskey and he downed it in one gulp. She hooked her arm in his as they headed across the backyard toward the stable. She smiled slyly to herself, knowing that she had slipped pills into Nick's drink and he hadn't even suspected anything. Soon, the real fun would begin.

Maggie was ready by seven thirty. She paced the foyer, anxious to leave but hoping that the rain would let up first. When it showed no signs of doing any such thing, she searched the coat closet for her umbrella, grabbed her keys, and ran down the sidewalk to the truck.

She panicked for a second when the engine sputtered, but it soon revved to life. During the short drive, she had drastic questions flowing through her mind, none of which she had the answers to. What would Nick say when he saw her? Would he be glad, or would he perhaps be irritated that he hadn't known she was coming? Would she be dressed appropriately?

Finally, she decided once and for all to push all negative thoughts aside. She was on her way and she wasn't turning back. If she were in Nick's position, she would be thrilled to see him show up unexpectedly. She decided that he would feel the same.

Her stomach tightened in knots, however, when she pulled onto Rockingham Lane and saw a black Expedition parked in the driveway. She pulled the rusty truck in next to it, feeling strangely out of place.

She checked her makeup in the mirror, took a deep breath, and opened the truck door. Although the rain had finally slowed to a drizzle, she opened her umbrella, not wanting to mess her hair or her outfit. She sidestepped several large puddles of rainwater as she headed toward the massive oak door. Once she stood squarely in front of it, she paused to take a deep breath before she reached out a shaky finger and rang the bell.

Within seconds, it seemed, the door was opened and Patricia stood towering above her. She smiled warmly. "Well, well, I've been expecting you. Come on in."

Maggie smiled hesitantly and stepped into the foyer. She slipped off her shoes, not wanting to dirty the floors.

"Come in to the study," Patricia said. "There's someone I want you to meet."

Maggie did as she was instructed, following quietly behind Patricia. She stepped onto white plush carpet inside the study. Looking around, she realized that the room must have belonged to Nick's father. Somehow she had missed this room during her tour of the house. It was decorated with cherry furniture, complete with a massive roll top desk. Pictures and certificates hung around the room. The walls were painted an earthy green, with white chair rail and crown molding, creating an interesting contrast. Heavy, expensive looking drapes hung from the two double windows.

A middle-aged distinguished looking gentleman with graying hair was sitting in a burgundy wingback chair sipping on a drink. He stood as soon as he saw Maggie and extended his hand.

"Jim Mason, this is Maggie Clark. She's a friend of Nick's." Patricia casually made the introductions.

"Pleased to meet you, Mr. Mason," Maggie said with a smile. *And I'm more than just a friend of Nick's,* she wanted to add, but didn't.

"The pleasure is all mine. And please call me Jim."

Maggie nodded at him, and an awkward silence followed. She got the feeling that she was interrupting something. After a brief moment, she asked, "Where's Nick?"

"Where did they get off to?" Jim asked Patricia as he took a sip of his drink.

Patricia shrugged. "Out back, somewhere. Try the barn or the stable. It's raining, so they couldn't have gone too far on foot."

"Um...who is 'they'?" Maggie's voice was soft and barely audible.

"Jim's daughter Natalie. Nick didn't tell you? The two of them go way back," Patricia said with a knowing smile and a flip of her hand. "Anyway, head on out there. The lights are on, so you shouldn't have any problem seeing. Would you like us to walk you out?"

Maggie, feeling a bit uncomfortable, shifted her weight from one foot to the other. The thought of Nick being out back somewhere, in the dark, with a girl that he hadn't mentioned made her feel...well, she wasn't sure *how* it made her feel. She didn't like it, she knew that much. A knot formed in the pit of her stomach.

She realized suddenly that Mrs. Winters and Jim were staring at her, waiting for a response. "Oh, no." She shook her head. "That's okay. I'll manage."

She said goodbye, then stepped into her shoes before heading out. She decided to go out the front door and walk around. She took her umbrella along as well, although she really didn't need it. It had completely stopped raining.

The rain had cooled the air considerably, and she shuddered faintly as the wind whipped through her hair. She pulled her light jacket a little more snugly around her body. The moon was almost totally obscured by the thick clouds, and if it weren't for the bright outdoor lighting around the back of the house, Maggie wouldn't have been able to see much at all. Her feet squished in a few marshy areas of the yard, and she sighed at the thought of what her shoes must look like.

She made it to the stable and noticed that the north door was ajar. Taking a deep breath, she headed toward the open entryway to see if anyone was inside. She felt a little silly, actually, creeping around in the dark like this, wearing her best dress. All day she had pictured arriving at the door and Nick answering it, surprised to see her and excitedly introducing her to everyone sitting around the table.

Not once, in thinking about the events of this evening, had she imagined that it would have worked out this way. Sighing and feeling a little discouraged, she reached the cement area at the end of the stable and stomped her feet to rid them of excess mud. She inched closer toward the door, and a large bolt of lightening shot across the dark sky, causing the night to brighten momentarily. It was soon followed by a huge crash of thunder, and Maggie jumped even though she had expected it.

Taking another deep breath to calm her frazzled nerves, Maggie opened the door a little further in order to squeeze in. Although the hinges appeared rusty, the door didn't make a sound. She allowed her eyes a moment to adjust to the dim lighting within. A small lamp was burning in a far corner, and as she started to inch forward she heard a sound. *What in the world was that?*

She stopped in her tracks, waiting to see if she heard anything further. Her heart was leaping in her chest. Maybe she should just leave. Just go home and wait to see Nick tomorrow.

No, she told herself. *Just keep going.*

She took a few more steps, anxious to find Nick but for some reason not compelled to call his name. She made her way slowly down the corridor, and all at once her breath caught, her hand went to her mouth, and she stifled a scream at the sight before her eyes.

Nick was lying on a bed of straw, straddled by a beautiful redhead. Although she couldn't see Nick's face from the angle she was standing, there was no doubt that it was him. The girl above him was obviously naked, her back to Maggie. A quilt surrounded her waist, but there was no question as to what was going on.

Nick's shirt was unbuttoned and spread apart, and although Maggie couldn't see anything of him from the waist down, she didn't need to in order to realize that he was naked as well.

Tears welled up in her eyes, and although she tried to move, tried to run, she couldn't. Her feet were planted firmly on the floor, and she was unable to think of anything rational at the moment.

So this is why Nick didn't want me around. What a stupid fool I've been!

She held her breath as she watched the two of them in action. The girl leaned over and kissed Nick, her beautiful hair falling across her face and his.

"Oh, Nick, I've missed you so much," the girl breathed.

A soft moan escaped Nick's lips, and his hands went to her waist.

Maggie decided that she had seen enough. She turned and ran, making little noise but not trying to be exceptionally quiet either. The rain had begun coming down hard again, and the ground was slippery. Not bothering to open her umbrella, she tore across the yard toward the driveway. Maggie lost her balance once and slid, smearing mud all over her dress and scraping her knee. She was thankful, at least, that she had thought to keep her keys in her jacket pocket so that she didn't have to ring the doorbell and face Mrs. Winters. If she wasn't already humiliated enough, having Mrs. Winters seeing her looking unkempt and distraught would have been the final straw.

By the time she reached the truck, her hair was plastered to her head. Her clothes, muddy and soaked, clung to her body. She shivered as she jumped in the truck and started it. Luckily it turned right over, and Maggie wasted no time in spinning out of the driveway, away from the only man she'd ever loved.

CHAPTER 20

Later, Maggie would recall that she didn't remember a single detail about the drive home. Her tears fell as rapidly as the rain on the windshield. Her heart continued to pound in her chest. Her knuckles, tightly gripping the steering wheel, were completely devoid of color. She had an assortment of emotions that she was feeling, from anger, to sadness, to denial, to embarrassment, and back to anger again.

"How could I have been so *stupid*?!" she cried aloud as she blindly wiped at her tears. "How could I not have known that something was going on?" She pounded on the steering wheel with her fist as she shouted the words.

She pulled briskly into the driveway, opened the door, and made a beeline for the house. Another lightening bolt lit up the gray sky, this one a little closer. She quickly unlocked the front door and proceeded to peel her pasted on clothes from her body inside the small foyer, leaving them in a heap.

She realized, then, just how tired and weary she felt. Her eyes burned from the tears, her head throbbed from the stress and tension, and her heart...well, her heart was broken. Just when she thought she could cry no more tears, Maggie once again broke down, her entire body shaking from the sobs that wracked her body. She cried for the love she had lost and for the Nick she thought she knew, now realizing that she hadn't really known him at all.

Sighing heavily, her shoulders sagging, Maggie climbed the stairs to the bathroom and ran warm water in the tub. Funny, she thought, just a couple of hours ago she had done the same thing. Not once had she thought that her evening would have ended like this.

After soaking for a bit, Maggie toweled off and wrapped herself in a thick, terry robe. Tired yet unable to sleep, she went downstairs and made herself a cup of hot chocolate. Outside, the rain had let up some, and the wind began to howl. A tree branch scraped eerily against the window and Maggie shuddered at the sound.

Turning off all the lights in the house except for a small lamp in the living room, Maggie climbed into an overstuffed chair and tucked her feet under her, her mug of hot chocolate in hand. Her mind felt numb.

She played the past few months over and over in her mind, and not once could she come up with anything unusual that Nick might have said. The only thing that troubled her was his behavior the past few days, before he told her that he would have to cancel their weekend plans. *Maybe he was trying to think of a way to break it off then*, Maggie thought, *but he didn't know how...it was just easier for him to start by breaking our weekend date.*

The tears began to fall again, and Maggie bit her lower lip to try and stop them. Of course it didn't work. They poured like a faucet, and Maggie put her head down on her knees and gave way to every emotion that she was feeling, her shoulders shaking violently with each sob.

Several hours later, just as the sun began to rise, Maggie finally drifted off into a dreamless, yet restless, sleep.

Nick awoke sometime after dawn, feeling tired and confused. He sat up quickly, and his hands immediately went to his head. It throbbed like it had been beaten with a hammer. It took him a moment to realize where he was. *The stable?* What was going on?

He sat up and brushed the itchy straw off of him, realizing for the first time that his shirt was unbuttoned and un-tucked. He checked his watch. Seven thirty five. *I slept here all night?*

Perplexed, he tried to piece together events from the night before. He remembered having dinner...and having a drink or two. *Oh, no. That must be it.* He sighed heavily and rubbed his eyes. He'd obviously had too much to drink.

He tried to stand, and swayed momentarily, feeling dizzy and lightheaded. He caught himself, then straightened. What else had happened? He had the feeling that something bad had been on his mind last evening, but his thoughts were fuzzy and he couldn't quite put his finger on what it was.

Natalie. Her name hit him like a ton of bricks, like a punch in the stomach. He remembered her getting a drink for him, following him out. He vaguely remembered sitting down on the straw when he got to the stable, and that was as far as his memory went. Surely nothing had happened between the two of them? He had fought her off all day, he remembered that, but wouldn't he remember if something physical had happened last night? The thought made him shudder. He felt physically ill.

He sighed heavily and sat back down on the bale of straw, burying his face in his hands. *What happened out here last night?* As much as it hurt to think, he tried desperately to remember any detail. Anything at all.

The attempt was futile. He couldn't remember a thing.

Standing again, this time slowly, he started to make his way back to the house. Hopefully Natalie would be gone, along with her father. Then he would be free to shower, and go and see Maggie...

We can be together, now... Nick smiled in spite of his raging hangover. It was over, the little deal he had made with his mother. He and Maggie could now live their lives in peace. The thought of it made him walk a little faster toward the house. Ignoring his pounding head, he took the stairs two at a time, anxious to shower and get over to see Maggie as soon as possible.

Maggie awoke to distant noises. She yawned and stretched her aching legs. Her neck hurt from sleeping in such an awkward position. She heard the noise again. Was someone knocking at the door?

She rubbed her eyes and glanced at the mantle clock. Not even nine o'clock in the morning. *It must be one of Grandma's friends*, she thought, forgetting that she was gone this weekend. Stretching again as she stood, she looked down and realized that she was still in her bathrobe. She took a quick peek in the hallway mirror and was greeted with red, swollen eyes and a head-full of disheveled hair.

"Great," she muttered out loud.

The knock came again, louder this time.

"Maggie, are you in there? Open up."

Maggie, barefoot, froze in her tracks. There was no mistaking the voice: it belonged to Nick. She started to panic; the familiar racing heart once again started up in her chest. *What is he doing here?*

She took a deep breath and paced back and forth in the hallway, pounding her small fist into the palm of her opposite hand. Should she open the door? Ignore him and pretend that she wasn't home? She clenched and unclenched her fists in nervous frustration, trying to quickly think of a solution.

The knock came again. This time even louder.

"Maggie?" Nick's voice pleaded. "Are you in there? C'mon, get up."

Maggie peeked out the front window. Nick stood facing the door, dressed in faded blue jeans and a burgundy button-down shirt, his hands in his pockets. His hair was damp. He looked worried. Or concerned. *Or guilty.*

Maggie debated about what to do for another moment. Finally, she eased open the door, leaving the security chain in place.

"Yes?" she said abruptly. Her heart ached to reach out and touch him, but she had to force herself to remain strong. *Think about what he's done*, she told herself. *He's played you for a fool.*

There was no mistaking the hurt on his face. "What do you mean 'yes'?" He laughed slightly and shrugged his shoulders. "I came to pick you up. My company is gone…let's go somewhere."

Maggie held his gaze without responding one way or another.

"What's wrong with you?" Nick asked. "Hey, have you been crying?" He reached quickly through the door and tried to grab her arm, but Maggie stepped back swiftly, her body completely out of his reach.

"Just go away, Nick." Maggie was glad that she remained within the shadows of the house so that Nick couldn't see the fresh tears or the swollen eyes. "Please…just go away." She willed her voice to remain calm and steady.

"Nick's face flushed in frustration. "How can you just ask me to go away? What's this all about?" His voice sounded desperate. He was close to the crack in the door, trying his best to peer in and get a look at Maggie.

"Nick...it's over, okay? That's what this is about. Obviously you and I just weren't meant to be together. You made your choice yesterday." It took all of Maggie's strength, all of her will, to make her voice sound strong. She held on to the wall to keep her body upright.

Nick felt like he had been punched in the stomach, as if all of the air in his lungs had been knocked out. *But I was doing it for you...for us!* He realized, now, how silly that sounded. Why hadn't he been honest with Maggie from the start, regarding his mother? Why hadn't he declined his mother's offer when she had presented the deal to him? It had seemed like the perfect solution at the time...but now...

"But, Maggie...I thought I explained that to you. It was just one day. If it meant that much to you, I wouldn't have canceled our date, all you had to do was say the word..."

"Enough, Nick." Maggie had to recall the image that she had seen last night in order to maintain her anger level. She wanted to open the door and collapse into Nick's arms, but she couldn't do that. She may be a lot of things, but she wasn't a pushover. Her survival instincts kicked in to high gear. "Obviously, being with your *company* was much more important." She said these last words with as much sarcasm as she could muster.

Nick's eyes burned from confusion. A heavy lump sat in his throat. Where was this coming from? Maggie had been fine, or so he thought, when he last saw her on Friday. What could have happened between now and then?

"Maggie, please. Don't do this. I'm sorry. You don't know how sorry I am." His voice was strained, pleading. "Please, let me explain. I can make this up to you!" His tone was desperate, but it was like talking to a brick wall.

"Just remember, Nick, that you did this to yourself." With that,

SIMPLE THINGS

Maggie quickly slammed the door before Nick could react, locking the deadbolt. She leaned against it and slid down slowly until she was sitting on the floor. She covered her face with both hands and began to sob silently, not wanting Nick to hear.

Immediately, Nick began pounding on the door.

"Maggie! Don't you do this! Open this door!" He paced the front porch, punched his fist into his hand, knocked some more. There was no response.

Frustrated and hurt, he jumped in his truck and sat there for a few moments, trying to collect his thoughts. This made no sense. Something happened to change her...but what? He jumped out of the truck again and beat loudly on the door one more time for emphasis.

When it was obvious that she wasn't going to open the door again, Nick once again headed to his truck, feeling confused and rejected. He backed out of the driveway slowly, watching the windows of the house for any activity, any movement. There was none.

He put the truck in to gear and spun out of the driveway, his mind swimming with confusion and unanswered questions.

CHAPTER 21

The rest of the day passed by in a blur for Nick. He drove around town, unable to go home and face his mother. Surely she would want to know why he wasn't spending the day with Maggie, as Natalie was long gone and he was free to date Maggie as he wished. He just couldn't deal with that right now, the questions she would ask would be hurtful, he was sure.

The rain had stopped sometime during the night, but the sky was still threatening to spill at any moment. The wind was strong, making it seem unusually cool for this time of year. Nick didn't seem to notice or care. He left his window down, the bitter air stinging his face.

He drove for hours, unaware of anything, his mind numb and his body on auto-pilot. For the life of him, he couldn't imagine what had happened to change Maggie. Her tone was so abrupt. It was also obvious, although he hadn't been able to get a good look at her, that she had been crying.

What could have happened?

The question continued to nag him. He drove past her house once again later in the day, but the truck was gone. He didn't bother to knock on the door...he knew that Lily was out of town, and that if the truck was gone, then Maggie was too.

He sat in the driveway for at least a half an hour, maybe longer. He stared at the weathered porch, the old rockers with the chipping paint and the swing that he had spent countless hours sitting on, Maggie by his side.

He stared at the beautiful flower-beds filled with impatiens and pansies, and remembered helping Maggie to weed them on more than one occasion.

He glanced to the old barn, and thought about the time he had chased Maggie around and around it after she had squirted him with the water hose.

In spite of his pain, he managed a small smile. He had so many good memories with Maggie. He had fully expected to spend the rest of his life with her. And now...well, now he didn't know what to think, where to go from here. His heart was shattered, his hopes and dreams along with it.

Sighing deeply, he reached down and started the ignition. Maybe Maggie had been okay about him spending the day with company at first, but after spending the day alone, obviously she had had plenty of time to think about it and she had grown resentful.

That's the only logical explanation he could come up with.

Nick backed slowly out of the driveway. He wished there was something, *anything*, that he could do to make it up to her.

For the next day or so, Nick tried incessantly to contact Maggie. He called and left messages, stopped by and tried to get her to open the door, but nothing he did worked. He stopped by the diner on Tuesday, after Lily was back and it was open for business again. To his surprise, he was greeted at the counter by an older woman that he hadn't met before.

"May I help you?"

Nick looked around over her shoulder for any sign of Maggie and stuffed his hands nervously into his front pockets. "Uh...is Maggie here?"

The older woman shook her head. "No, I'm sorry. She took ill, so I'm here helping her grandmother out. Would you like to speak with Lily, by chance?"

Nick bit his lower lip, removed his hands from his pockets, and crossed his arms. He nodded slowly. "Yes, please."

After a moment, Lily emerged from the back, wiping her hands on her apron. "Well, look who's here," she said slowly. "I guess you heard that Maggie stayed home."

Nick nodded. "I...I just want you to know that..."

Lily stopped him abruptly by raising her hand, palm side out.

Her eyes remained warm, but she was straightforward in what she had to say.

"I don't know what happened between you two, and I'm not sure that I want to," she began. "But I do know that Maggie has her mind made up about you staying away from her. She didn't tell me what's going on...she's always been one to keep things to herself." She shook her head slightly, then continued. "Maybe she'll come around, maybe she won't. But you need to please respect her wishes...quit calling, quit showing up unannounced." Lily reached a weathered hand out and patted Nick's shoulder. "If this is meant to be, all of this will work out in the end anyway."

Nick looked down at his feet before slowly making eye contact with Lily. "That's just it...I don't understand what happened...I had to break one date, and I thought she was fine, and then..."

"Well, maybe that's it," Lily interrupted, offering an explanation. "Her mother used to break dates with her all the time, and she started to grow a wall around her when it came to people." She paused, thinking, then shrugged her shoulders. "Who knows, maybe it has something to do with that. But it's not my business. Maggie will come around in her own time. All I can do is ask you to stay away and let her deal with it in her own way." Lily tried to say the words forcefully, yet with kindness all the same.

Sadly, Nick nodded, then looked away. "Okay. You're right." He started to walk toward the door, then turned back. "It was nice getting to know you, Lily."

Lily simply nodded in response, and with that, Nick was gone.

After Nick left, Lily called her granddaughter on the phone to let her know what had happened. After repeating the conversation, Lily took a deep breath. "Maybe you should talk to him, at least once, before he goes," Lily said, unsure of what kind of response she would get. There was none. Maggie had simply sighed, said goodbye, and hung up.

After talking to her grandmother, Maggie thought more and more

about what she had said. Maybe she should talk to him, just once. Tell her what she really thought of him.
   No, she thought. Seeing him again would just make it harder.
   Still, the more she thought about it, the more she wondered if she should. Although it was obvious what she had seen, it would be nice to hear his explanation. *Get real*, she thought again. *There is no explaining what I saw.*
   Sighing, Maggie went upstairs to her room and took out a piece of lavender stationary. She would write what she was feeling, then drop it by Nick's house. She doubted he would be home in the middle of the day, anyway. Stretching out across her bed, she began to write.

   Two hours later, feeling nervous and unsure of herself, Maggie pulled into Nick's driveway. She had planned on leaving the note in the mailbox, but she wasn't sure if the mail had already been picked up for the day. Since she didn't see Nick's truck, Maggie stepped out slowly and walked the familiar sidewalk to the front door, with images of the last time she had been here flashing through her mind. She forced the thoughts away, took a deep breath, and rang the bell.
   Within minutes, Mrs. Winters opened the door, looking startled to see Maggie. "Oh, my, you surprised me," she said, eyeing her curiously. "Shouldn't you be at work?"
   Maggie shook her head slowly. "I wasn't feeling well."
   "Oh." Mrs. Winters responded as she anxiously clutched a strand of pearls hanging from her neck. "Well, Nicholas isn't here."
   "Well, that's okay," Maggie said with a small shrug. "I just wanted to leave something for him." She reached into her purse and pulled out a lavender envelope. "Would it be possible for you to give this to Nick for me?"
   Mrs. Winters smiled warmly although quivering on the inside. "Why, I'd be glad to. He was out running a few errands, getting last minute things he needs for school," she said with a smile. "But he should be back real soon." After a minute, she hesitantly asked, "Would you like to come in?"
   Maggie shook her head. "No, thank you, Mrs. Winters. If you

could just give him that, I would appreciate it." With that, she turned and slowly headed back the way she had come.

Maggie had no sooner driven away when Patricia began pacing the floor. She thought that everything was over between Nick and Maggie. After talking with Natalie, and after she had peered out the window in time to see Maggie peel out of the driveway on Saturday night, she was sure that Maggie would never want to have anything to do with Nick again.

And of course Nick hadn't been acting like himself. He was quiet, withdrawn...more so than usual. She knew that he might be miserable right now, but one day, she was sure, he would thank her for this.

But then again, he could *never* know that she was the one responsible for what had happened between Nick and Maggie.

Sighing, Patricia walked into the study and opened the top drawer of the roll-top desk. Pulling out a gold letter opener, she sharply slit the end of the envelope, greedily pulling out the folded paper inside and devouring the words quickly.

Dear Nick,

I'm not sure how to describe to you what I'm feeling right now. I have spent sleepless nights lately, my mind only on thoughts of you, of us, and what could have possibly gone wrong. I know I may not be perfect, but I can't think of anything I could have done to deserve this. Anyway, enough of that for now. I am writing mainly because I don't want you to go away with out us speaking, without us getting everything out in the open. I know you've tried to contact me a lot lately, but I just haven't been ready to face you until now. So I'm asking you to meet me tonight, at eight o'clock sharp, at the cabin. Our place, remember? If you choose not to show up, I will understand, and I will take it to mean that you and I are completely over. But if you decide to go, I will be there waiting.

Maggie

SIMPLE THINGS

After reading the letter, a Patricia's stomach knotted up with the realization that Maggie and Nick could easily talk, put everything together, and discover what she'd done.

She couldn't, and *wouldn't*, let that happen.

Quickly, Patricia fed the letter through the paper shredder, cutting it to tiny bits. Then, as if that weren't enough, she grabbed the remaining evidence and flushed it down the toilet, hoping to finally be rid of Maggie Clark forever.

CHAPTER 22

Three months had passed since Maggie had last seen Nick, since her heart had been ripped away. The fall weather had slowly changed to winter, and the leaves, once beautiful shades of orange, red, and yellow, had slipped briskly from the trees like Nick had slipped from Maggie's life.

Bare branches now stood where the leaves once had, large arms reaching for the gray winter sky. Early December, the winter was one of the coldest they had had in Cedar Creek for several years. The higher elevation of the area made the cold air thin, burning, almost, as it was inhaled.

Slowly, Maggie had begun to emerge from her shell. Although she still hadn't told her grandmother what had happened with Nick, Maggie still thought about it, though not constantly like she had in the beginning. She hurt the most when she remembered waiting outside the cabin that night, expecting Nick to show up, coming to the realization that the two of them were completely over.

Lately, she had started acting more like herself, something her grandmother had just mentioned the day before when Maggie offered to help bake pies in the kitchen for the Christmas festival that would be held that weekend.

Her grandmother had hired a young woman in the diner, in her mid-twenties with a young son. Her family was new in town, and she had been looking to find something she could do in the mornings while her son was in school. It was the perfect arrangement for all of them. She ended up being there part-time, helping to cover the lunch period. Maggie had grown to be friends with her, and spent an occasional evening at Rachel's house with her husband Ron and son Luke. Maggie enjoyed her time with them, and it helped her to slowly get her mind off of Nick, although not completely.

The weekend of the Christmas festival, Maggie was busy helping her grandmother gather her pies and other baked goods that she would be selling at a small stand. The doorbell rang just as Maggie was setting a few things down in the foyer.

"Get that, will you, honey?" her grandmother yelled from the kitchen. "It's probably Ruth Ann...she was going to stop by and help."

Wiping her hands on her jeans, Maggie reached for the knob and pulled the door open, a blast of cold winter air hitting her forcefully in the face. She gasped, speechless, and stared back at the person before her.

Standing on her front porch was a beautiful redhead. The same redhead that had haunted her in her dreams, her nightmares, ever since she had seen her that night with Nick in the stable all those months ago.

Maggie was frozen, mouth open, unsure of what to say. After a moment, the girl staring back at her spoke.

"You must be Maggie." Her voice was calm and steady.

Maggie wanted to slam the door, but her muscles wouldn't budge. She found herself responding by nodding slowly.

"My name is Natalie. I need to talk to you." She paused, then asked, "May I come in?"

At that point, Maggie seemed to come to her senses. She straightened her posture and once again shook her head. "I'm sorry, but I don't think so. I really don't think we have anything to discuss." She tried to shut the door, but the effort was quickly blocked.

"Please." Natalie's eyes pleaded. "This is hard enough for me. I wouldn't be here if it wasn't important."

Something in Natalie's tone made Maggie release her grip on the door, and it was easily pushed aside. Maggie stepped back and allowed Natalie to step inside the small foyer. Finding her voice, Maggie spoke. "Follow me."

Natalie followed closely behind Maggie as she was led into the living room. Maggie turned slowly to face Natalie. "I don't know what all of this is about, but I want you to make it quick." Her breathing was rapid, her pulse swift. It took immense effort to speak in a civil tone.

Natalie took a deep breath and sat down on the edge of the couch. "Look, this isn't easy for me, I've already told you that. But please, just hear me out." Her eyes focused on Maggie's. "Just give me a few minutes, okay?"

Reluctantly, Maggie nodded slowly, then backed up to an armchair and sat down, arms crossed. Her eyes narrowed at Natalie as she began to speak.

"What you think happened with Nick that night…well, it didn't really happen." Natalie said the words quickly, afraid that she would lose her nerve and not get the words out.

"What do you mean?" Maggie's brow furrowed.

Natalie looked away, stared out the window, hoping that it would make it easier to say what she needed to if she wasn't looking Maggie in the eye. She closed her eyes and sighed. "Just what I said. Nick was set up." She paused briefly before adding, "By his mother."

Maggie's gasp was audible in the quiet room. "I…I don't understand. Why would she do such a thing?"

Natalie clasped her hands together and leaned forward in her seat. "Patricia never wanted you and Nick together. She wanted him to date someone…well, she just didn't want him to date *you*."

"I see." Maggie inhaled sharply and bit her lower lip, fighting off tears that were threatening to come. *Don't cry in front of her,* she told herself.

Natalie continued, telling Maggie all of the details of the arrangement Patricia made with Nick. "I was there as a distraction, to get his mind off of you. And of course Patricia managed to get you to agree to come over, which made everything work in her favor."

Maggie tried to digest everything that she was being told. "But what about the stable…I saw you two…"

Natalie shook her head. "No, you *thought* you knew what was going on, but you were wrong. Nick was fully clothed under the blanket. He passed out and had no clue what was happening. When you arrived at the house, Patricia called me on my cell phone to let me know you were on your way out to the stable." She paused to take a breath. "The rest was easy."

Maggie, still speechless, shook her head, her mind going back to that night. Her eyes narrowed at Natalie. "Well tell me this…how did you know that it would work? I mean, how did you manage to lure Nick out there?" Maggie didn't want to imagine that Nick had *wanted* to go out to the stable alone with Natalie.

Natalie rubbed her temples and answered slowly. "He had had a few drinks that night. I invited myself along against his wishes. I managed to slip something that my friend gave me into his drink right before we went out to the stable. It was just supposed to make him drowsy, but I guess with the alcohol already on board, it really knocked him out."

Maggie jumped to her feet in one swift motion. "You *drugged* him?!"

"I know, I know. It was stupid. I just promised Patricia that I would make it work. That's the only thing I could think of to do."

Maggie sat back down, wanting to hear the rest of the story, yet disgusted by it all the same. "Does Nick know about any of this?"

Natalie shook her head. "I think he suspects something, but can't prove it. He won't have anything to do with me. He hasn't really spoken to his mother, either, since he went back to college. Evidently he was heartsick when you wouldn't have anything to do with him. His mother was thrilled, however."

Maggie closed her eyes and tried to slowly control her breathing. "He must not be too upset. I left a letter asking him to meet me…" All of a sudden, she came to the realization of what had happened. Natalie nodded in response.

"Right. Patricia destroyed the letter. She told me about it."

All at once, the hurt and the confusion that Maggie had felt for the past several months melted away. It hurt her, yes, that Nick's mother had gone through extreme measures to keep Nick away from Maggie. *But Nick hasn't done anything wrong.*

Maggie frowned, however, when she realized what he must be going through too. He had no idea why she had broken off their relationship, no understanding as to what it was he supposedly did. Maggie felt terrible that she hadn't trusted Nick. Tears burned her eyes and she wiped them blindly with the back of her hand.

Natalie took that as her cue to leave. Standing slowly, she spoke to Maggie once again. "I guess I'll be going now. I've left you with a lot to think about." She turned and headed for the front door, keys in hand.

"Wait."

Natalie turned back and faced Maggie, not knowing what kind of reaction to expect.

Maggie took a deep breath before she spoke. "I just want to know one thing. Why, after all these months of not saying anything, did you decide to tell the truth now?"

Natalie waited a few minutes before she answered, trying to collect her thoughts. "I'm not sure. I've always had a thing for Nick, although the feeling was never returned. Patricia knew that and wanted to use it to her advantage. And I'm not placing all of the blame on her, either...I know that I didn't have to go through with it. I thought at first that it was no big deal, that it was payment for a favor I owed Patricia from a while back. But the more I thought about it, the worse I felt." She paused before continuing. "Patricia will be furious when she finds out I told. She'll probably never want to speak to me again."

Maggie sighed. "I appreciate you telling me the truth. Although I don't understand exactly *why* you would do something so intentionally cruel and hurtful."

Natalie shrugged her shoulders. "I don't know, either. And I don't expect you forgive me. But believe it or not, I haven't been able to forget about it since it happened." She paused and looked away. "I *do* want to change the person I've become. And I thought this would be a good place to start."

Maggie, in spite of the anger she had felt earlier, felt herself actually feeling sorry for Natalie. She attempted a small smile before speaking. "I will forgive you...one day. But there's no way I can ever forget what's happened. Three months of my life with Nick have been lost...and for what?" Maggie paused, not really expecting

an answer to her rhetorical question.
   Natalie nodded. "I know, you're right." There was nothing else to say.
   Natalie turned then and headed slowly back toward the door. She turned around once her hand was on the doorknob. "By the way...Nick is on his way home for the weekend. He should be home now, in fact." She then slipped out silently as Maggie remained in her seat, her mind swirling with emotions and the news she'd just been given.

CHAPTER 23

In the moments that followed Natalie's departure, Maggie's mind raced, trying to fill in all of the gaps within her memory. She went back to the times she had been around Patricia, the time that Patricia had called her on the phone to invite her to dinner...as a *surprise* to Nick. It all made sense now...although she still didn't understand it.

She rose from the chair and paced the living room, pausing once to peek through the blinds at the icy sky. She felt horrible that she had jumped to conclusions about Nick and Natalie...but it was so *realistic*. All of it. She was only protecting herself by shutting Nick out in those days that had followed. It was a defense mechanism that she had grown accustomed to using over the years.

But will Nick be willing to forgive me for my lack of trust in him?

She was still staring out the window when her grandmother spoke up quietly behind her. "Maggie? You okay, honey?"

Maggie withdrew her thumbnail that she was absentmindedly chewing on from the corner of her mouth. She looked over her shoulder at her grandmother, a blank look in her eyes. "Hmmm?"

Her grandmother walked a little closer, wringing her hands. "I'm sorry, but I couldn't help but overhear what was said in here." Nervously, she added, "I'm afraid I haven't been completely honest with you, either."

Maggie turned and faced her grandmother, her eyes full of questions. Sighing, she tucked her hair behind each ear. "What is it? I've already had one bomb dropped on me today."

Her grandmother shook her head slightly. "Oh, no, it's nothing quite like that." She sat down on the sofa and patted the seat beside her. Maggie reluctantly sat down on the spot indicated by her grandmother. "I should have told you back when you first became involved with Nick, but I didn't want to cause trouble."

SIMPLE THINGS

Maggie sat silently, watching and waiting for her grandmother to continue.

"Your mother and Nick's mother knew each other growing up. And to say that they weren't exactly friends would be quite an understatement. You see, your mother was wild and outgoing, always catching the attention of young men, as I may have told you before. She even managed to catch the attention of Patricia's boyfriend...who would later become your father."

Maggie gasped. "Mrs. Winters used to date my *father?*"

Her grandmother nodded. "I'm afraid so. She had a fit when she found out that your mother stole him from her. She became irate, calling all hours of the night, leaving nasty notes on the door. It got pretty ugly." She sighed loudly and dropped her shoulders. "Eventually things died down and your mother moved out of town with your father. Patricia seemed to change and got married to Michael, who was a dear soul. She became prominent in the community and so-forth, even hosting charity fund-raisers from time to time. I haven't had any encounter with her for years, and I thought maybe, just maybe, she was truly a different person." She shrugged her shoulders and squeezed Maggie's hand. "That's why I chose not to say anything to you...I didn't want to give you the wrong impression of her...I wanted you to develop your own. I just wish, now, that I *had* said something. You might have had your eyes open for something like this to happen, instead of trusting her and letting her ruin your relationship with Nick."

Maggie's arms instinctively went around her grandmother's shoulders. "It's not your fault. Please don't think that it is." She pulled back. "Besides, who says that she's ruined things with Nick?" A small smile crossed her soft lips. "He's at home this weekend, and I'm going to see him." She raised her chin slightly in determination.

Her grandmother smiled and kissed Maggie on the cheek. "That's my girl."

Maggie nervously drove the few miles to Nick's house in her small used car that she had purchased the previous month. It wasn't the sports car she had always dreamed about, but it was reliable and definitely affordable.

Her hands gripped the wheel cautiously as she drove the familiar back roads. For a while after Nick first left, she used to drive by his house every few days or so, just hoping to get a glimpse of him, even though she knew he wouldn't be there. As time passed by, she drove by less and less frequently, and now that she thought about it, she couldn't remember the last time she'd driven past.

Before she knew it, she was turning onto Rockingham Lane, and her stomach tightened into one big knot. Her palms felt sweaty; her pulse accelerated and was throbbing in her temples. She tried to calm her breathing as she rounded a curve and saw Nick's truck parked in its customary spot in the driveway. She felt sick to her stomach yet excited at the same time.

What if Nick won't talk to me? What if he reacts the way I did the morning he stopped by the house? These thoughts, among others, washed through Maggie's mind as she pulled into the driveway and stepped out into the frigid air. She slammed the car door and took a deep breath before shakily walking the distance to the front door.

She hesitated once she reached it, and considered turning around and heading straight back to the safety of her car. She wasn't sure if she was emotionally up for this…everything had changed so quickly, so suddenly.

She thought, then, about Nick. She felt terrible for what he must have gone through. Pushing all insecurities away, she took a deep breath and reached out a trembling finger to ring the bell.

CHAPTER 24

After a few moments, the door was opened abruptly, and Nick stood in the foyer, those piercing blue eyes penetrating Maggie's. Neither one spoke or moved a muscle.

Maggie wondered what was going through Nick's mind as he stared back at her. *Maybe this wasn't such a good idea,* she thought to herself. *Maybe I should have called...or just stayed away. That might have been easier for the both of us.*

She cleared her throat, a demure look crossed her face, and she began by asking a simple question: "I bet you're wondering just what I'm doing on your doorstep, huh?" Her voice was low, soft.

Nick shook his head side to side. A look of surprise, and concern, lingered in his eyes. He smiled softly. "How've you been, Maggie?"

Maggie tried to smile back, but instead found tears welling up in the corners of her eyes. "Oh, Nick, I'm so sorry. Can you ever forgive me?" Her shoulders dropped, heavy with guilt, and she covered her face with both of her hands.

In an instant, Nick was out the front door, both arms wrapped around Maggie. He didn't know what this was all about, but it didn't matter...he hated to see Maggie upset...to see her cry was even worse.

He patted her back patiently while she sobbed on his shoulder, finally letting out all of the emotions that she had been holding back. He smoothed her hair as she pulled back from him. He then wiped her tears with his thumb, cradling her face in his masculine hand.

"Maggie, what is it? Please talk to me." Nick's voice was full of worry.

Through choked tears and sobs, Maggie tried to speak. "So sorry...I didn't trust you...all my fault..." She then broke down again, her shoulders shaking violently.

"Here, come in, we'll talk where it's warm." Nick spoke with a soft yet strong voice as he gently grabbed Maggie by the elbow to lead her inside.

Maggie was reluctant. "Is...is anyone else home?"

"No, it's just me." He nudged her forward once again. "Come on in. Let me get you something warm to drink."

Once inside, Nick removed Maggie's coat for her and hung it in the closet. She followed him to the kitchen and sat down, watching as he prepared two cups of hot tea. She wondered what he was thinking about her just showing up on his doorstep. It had been three months since she had turned her back on him, all because of a misunderstanding, yet he hadn't hesitated once to open the door to her, to welcome her back into his loving embrace.

Thinking about this made her feel even worse about herself. *How could I have treated him so badly?*

Once the tea was ready, Nick carefully set a cup in front of her before pulling a chair out for himself. He stared into Maggie's emerald eyes, eyes that were red-rimmed from crying. He reached over slowly and squeezed her hand.

"Talk to me," he said, his voice warm. "What brought you crying to my door?"

Maggie's head dropped down and the tears came again, pouring as if a faucet had been turned on. "I just feel so awful about everything," Maggie said finally, once the tears had begun to subside. She wiped her eyes with a tissue that Nick handed her, then slowly raised them to meet his.

She began to talk then, telling about her unexpected invitation to dinner that night not so long ago, about the discovery she had made in the stable, and finally, about Natalie's surprise visit that morning. Nick listened to all of it without responding, letting every horrible detail sink in. When she was finished, Nick let out a long, slow whistle.

"I *knew* it," he said, his jaw tightening into a tense contraction. "I knew she was involved somehow, but I couldn't do a damn thing to prove it." His eyes narrowed in concentration as he focused on nothing in particular, the wheels in his mind turning at an accelerated speed.

"I just feel so awful, Nick. I blew it with us. I didn't trust you, and I made a fool out of myself in the process of kicking you out of my life." Her delicate chin rose slightly to look at Nick; her eyes were still damp from the recent tears. "I don't expect you to forgive me easily...but I would do anything, *anything*, to make it up to you."

Nick shook his head and reached out to hold Maggie's hand. "If I had been honest with you from the start, none of this would have happened, anyway. She would have never been able to come between us like that had you known the truth."

Maggie's brow wrinkled in confusion. "What do you mean?"

Nick shrugged his shoulders gently. "Just that I tried to protect you from my mother by not telling you about how she really felt about you...about *us*. She would rather see me unhappy with someone that *she* chose for me than to see me with you." He shook his head. "I was embarrassed and didn't want to tell you the truth...I thought it was something I could just avoid. Boy, was I wrong."

He went on, then, to tell Maggie about the deal he had made with his mother. Maggie listened intently and reached over to squeeze Nick's hand.

"I wish you had told me, just so you didn't have to burden yourself with everything," Maggie said softly. "But I can't say that I blame you for what you did. My mother *always* did things to embarrass me when I was around her, and I found myself keeping secrets from others, too, because of it." She sighed and reached up to touch Nick's face. "But you could have told me, Nick. I would have understood."

Nick managed a small smile. "I know that, now, Maggie. It never works to keep secrets from the ones you love." He exhaled deeply. "You know, your grandfather was right."

Maggie gazed at him, an evident question in her eyes. "What do you mean?"

"The simple things *are* the most important in life." He gestured around the room with his hand. "These things...these material things...they mean nothing to me. I don't need money or wealth. As long as I have you in my life, then I'll be a happy *and* a rich man for

as long as I live."
　Their eyes met then and it was if time stood still. Nick stood and came around to Maggie, pulling her up to him. They stepped closer to each other until their bodies met, the heat passing from one to the next.
　Maggie's body trembled with anticipation as if it were the first time he had touched her. She closed her eyes slowly as he leaned down to kiss her. Her mouth felt like it was on fire from the touch of his lips, and as the kiss deepened, Maggie felt her body go limp in his arms. This, she knew, was how life was supposed to be.
　Nick moaned softly as he ran his fingers through Maggie's long blond hair. "Don't ever leave me again, Maggie. I couldn't bear it." He kissed her again, and pulled away long enough to breathe, "Marry me."
　Maggie's heart skipped a beat. A lump formed in her throat as she squeezed Nick tightly around his neck and closed her eyes, whispering her answer into his ear. "I will, Nick. I will."

EPILOGUE

A winter chill was in the air, and Maggie exhaled a visible breath as she stood on the back porch of her new home. She pulled her sweater a little closer around her while watching Nick finish stringing up the last of the Christmas lights, smiling to herself as she saw how carefully he tacked them in to place.

Nick glanced down from the ladder he was standing on and caught her watching him. He winked at her as he continued to work. Maggie giggled to him, then shouted: "Come on down, it's getting cold!" She rubbed her hands together quickly to warm them.

Nick finished the last strand before carefully backing down, pulling his work gloves off one at a time as he did so. Maggie's eyes twinkled as he came toward her and a warm glow flowed instantly through her body.

She couldn't help but think back and realize just how far the two of them had come, just how much their lives had changed...

After Maggie had accepted Nick's marriage proposal this time last year, they had decided to marry quickly and quietly, sparing anyone the opportunity to come between them again. They pledged their love for one another in a small Baptist church in nearby Chesterfield, with only Maggie's grandmother in attendance.

They honeymooned during Nick's Christmas vacation from college at the cabin, making love each night by a crackling fire, lights from the tiny tree that they had decorated together twinkling brightly.

Then, one day before Nick was due back at school, the two of them had gone together, hand in hand, to tell Nick's mother the news. Maggie's stomach had been in knots at the thought of what they were about to do, but she stood strong and faced the woman that had nearly destroyed her life with Nick.

Next to being without Nick, it had proved to be the hardest thing Maggie had ever done. Patricia had called her horrible names and had insisted that Nick get the marriage annulled. Nick, of course, had refused. In a most calm and even voice he had explained to his mother that he and Maggie were meant to be together, and that no one, her included, would ever come between them again.

With that, the two had strolled hand in hand out the door, leaving behind an astonished Patricia who, for once in her life, was at a loss for words.

Nick had graduated from college and joined a local building company. He specialized in refurbishing old homes, something that he had always wanted to do. His first major project was Lily's farmhouse, which made Lily and Maggie both extremely happy. Although it wasn't complete yet, he was overseeing the remodeling, happy with the results so far.

Nick had also designed the plans for the house Maggie and he now lived in. It was a modest three bedroom rancher, built just down the road from the cabin in a quiet and remote area near the winding creek. As stipulated in Nick's fathers will, Nick had received nearly fifty acres, as well as the cabin, upon his twenty-second birthday. Maggie had to pinch herself sometimes to realize that this was *her* life that she was living, and not something out of a fairy tale. She was thankful everyday for the miracle of Nick walking into the diner that spring evening. She knew, as well as she knew anything, that the two of them had been destined to fall in love, to be together forever.

Now, Maggie watched as Nick came toward her and her heart once again skipped a beat. She felt such love, such compassion, for this man that it almost hurt. She grinned as Nick's arms enveloped her into a warm embrace, his blue eyes sparking on the front porch, his breath visible in the cold mountain air. He reached down and patted her slightly protruding belly, now five months along with their baby girl. They planned on naming her Allyson, meaning *truthful*. She chose the name based on its meaning, a word that brought back many memories for Maggie, some of them painful. Truth, she and

Nick both now knew, was synonymous with the word love. To have one, you must have the other.

Maggie wondered to herself, as she stepped into the toasty family room of her home with Nick on her heels, just what to think about Patricia. On one hand Maggie despised her, yet on the other she felt pity. Someone must be truly miserable, she decided, to go through such extreme efforts to try and ruin a love as strong as the one Maggie and Nick had for one another. Just the other day, however, she had been baking bread in the kitchen when she thought she heard a car door slam. As she peeked out the front door, she saw Patricia's car speeding away. On the porch steps was a small wrapped baby gift with no card. Inside she found a tiny gold locket that had been Nick's when he was a baby. Maggie had smiled to herself. Maybe, just maybe, she was coming around.

As Nick stood beside her with his strong arm around her waist, he flipped on the switch that lit the entire yard. White and red flashing lights appeared, bathing Nick and Maggie in its warm glow. Maggie closed her eyes and took a deep breath. No matter what happened from now on, she knew that she would be fine. She reminded herself to never take Nick, or the simple things, for granted again.

Printed in the United States
702200001B